NO DIRECTION HOME

ON THE EDGE

BOOK 3

MIKE SHERIDAN

Editing by Felicia Sullivan

Proofreading by Laurel Kriegler

Cover art by Deranged Doctor Design

CHAPTER 1

Mason Bonner sat in the living room of his 35-foot Highland Ridge Roamer, the luxurious trailer left to him by Wasson Lodge's departed leader, a man by the name of Chris. A generous gift, Mason had joked at the time, considering the two had barely met.

Despite his comfortable living arrangements, however, Mason was in a foul mood, and had been for two straight days, ever since his hostage Ned Granger had been rescued and his friend and adviser Russ Willis captured in his place. Making matters worse, two of his crew had been killed in the process.

Anger and frustration gnawed at him while he came to terms with the dramatic turn of events. His girl, Tania, wisely stayed out of his way as much as possible, dutifully washing his clothes, preparing his meals, doing all she could to appease his ill humor.

At least fresh meat was back on the table, a welcome change from the soggy pasta dishes he'd endured for the past two weeks. Several of his men were experienced hunters, and returned to camp each day with venison and wild boar that was grilled every evening in large fire pits. Under normal circumstances, it would have put him in excellent spirits, but with his recent reversal of fortune, not even the succulent fresh meat could improve his mood. Mason wouldn't be happy until he got even with Rollins.

That wouldn't be easy. The sheriff now knew exactly how many men he had at his disposal, which was not the sixty he'd claimed, and he wasn't in the least intimidated by his threats. The information had almost certainly been extracted from Russ during his capture. Mason doubted it had taken much work. While cunning and sneaky, Russ wasn't exactly someone who had much going on in the bravery department, if that department even existed.

Nonetheless, at dawn that morning, Mason had led a team of eight men into Camp Benton's grounds in a daring bid to slip past their defenses. If he'd found out where they were holding Russ, perhaps he could have rescued him. Things hadn't gone well. The camp perimeter was heavily guarded, and he and his men had been spotted, then chased back with their tails between their legs under a barrage of heavy gunfire, worsening his mood even further.

Mason wasn't the type of person to sit back passively and just give up, however. After he cooled down, he began hatching a new plan to get even with the sheriff, something practical that stood a real chance of succeeding. A grim smile came to his lips as he played with a certain scheme in his mind.

His thoughts were interrupted by a light rap on the door. "Come in," he called out.

The door opened and Doney, his trusted bodyguard, stepped inside. Mason waved him over to where he sat on the sofa.

"What's up?"

Doney stared down at Mason a little uncertainly. With his recent dark moods, even Doney walked on eggshells around him. "Boss, the men just found Russ at the bottom of the driveway. He had a pillowcase over his head and four bullets in his chest."

Mason stared back at Doney expressionlessly. He'd been expecting the news of Russ's demise at any moment, though it hadn't occurred to him that the sheriff would callously dump his body like that. Rollins was more ruthless than he'd thought.

"Well, they executed him," he said in a flat tone. "Just like they said they would if we didn't pick up and leave here."

Doney appeared relieved that his boss hadn't erupted into yet another of his explosive rages. "What do you want us to do with him?"

Mason shrugged indifferently. He'd already moved on from Russ. He wasn't the sentimental type either. "Dump him in the forest. I'm told there's plenty of wolves around. They'll be happy to get a free meal."

A tight smile came to Doney's lips. Like the rest of Mason's crew, he'd made it apparent that he hadn't thought too much of Russ. "I'll see to it." He headed toward the door.

"Hey, Doney," Mason called after him. "When you're done, grab four men and report back to me. We're going to take a trip around the lake, see if we can't make some new friends."

"Friends?" Doney raised an eyebrow questioningly.

Mason grinned. "Yeah, you never know when they might come in useful. If they've got a boat, that'd be even better."

CHAPTER 2

In what used to be the YMCA staff lounge, the five members of the Benton Council sat around the table. Half an hour ago, Russ had been executed and his body dumped at the bottom of the Wasson Lodge driveway, a tit-for-tat retaliation on Rollins's part. Three days beforehand, Mason had dumped the bodies of several members of the Camp Knox group at the top of their drive, and he was sending the bandit a clear signal. If Mason wanted a brutal war between the two camps, he would get one.

"What now?" Henry Perter asked, peering nervously around the table. "Mason is sure to be pissed as hell. He's going to want revenge right away."

"We'll be ready for him, Hank," Ned Granger said confidently. "He's got less than twenty men. That's not enough to take this camp. No way in hell."

Perter appeared reassured by Granger's words. The two men had been good friends before the pandemic, and though nervous by nature, he'd never once shirked from his duties since his appointment to the council. Two days ago, when Kit Halpern discovered where Mason had been holding Granger captive, it had been Perter who was first to burst into the living room at Old Fort, killing both of Mason's guards.

"Maybe we should attack first," Mary Sadowski mused. "When Mason's least expecting it."

"Like when…tonight?" Bert Olvan asked, sitting next to her.

Sadowski nodded.

"Might be a better way to utilize Walter and his group," Granger said, rubbing his chin. "If we wait for Mason to attack, the whole thing could be over by the time they arrive. That's no use to anybody."

Thirty minutes ago, Walter and Cody had returned to their camp in the Alaculsy Valley. Seeing as they were responsible for Mason's presence at the Cohutta, the two had promised to help fight the bandit once Walter consulted with his group. Since the distance between the two camps was too great to maintain radio contact, Rollins had suggested that he and Walter meet that afternoon at the Harris Branch once Walter knew how many people he could commit to the cause. The Harris Branch was approximately the halfway point between the two camps.

Sadowski stared at Granger. "What makes you so sure he and his friends will show up when we need them?"

"He'll show," Granger said confidently. "Walter's not the sort to go back on his word. Question is, how many will agree to come with him."

"Cody will, for sure," Rollins said. "As for the others, we'll just have to wait and see. Remember, half their group knows nothing about Mason. It's not really their fight. Ned, if we were to attack tonight, how would we best use them?"

"We should get them to attack the lodge from the Devil's Point side of the peninsula," Granger replied. "Take the same route Mason used. Give him a taste of his own medicine."

Rollins turned to Sadowski. "You think our people are well-trained enough for an assault on the lodge? Defending our camp is one thing; going on the attack is another."

Sadowski nodded. "I think so. Besides, *you* were prepared to storm the lodge if need be when Ned was held captive, remember?"

Rollins put on a mock scowl. "Now, Mary, I told you not to tell Ned that. You'll give him a big head."

Granger chuckled. "I'll start working on a plan. If we're going to take the lodge, a good plan and the element of surprise will be crucial. John, remember those night vision glasses I showed you the other day? Well, they'll be just as useful in an attack."

Rollins nodded. On their second day at the camp, the two had toured its defenses. Afterward, Granger had shown him the five pairs of night vision glasses he'd picked up in Cleveland. "What time should we attack?"

Granger thought for a moment. "From what I saw, Mason and his men stay up pretty late. They like to drink…a lot. Three a.m. should be a good time." He looked around the table. "I don't think I need tell you, there'll be some fireworks tonight when this party gets going. Mary, have you drilled our three new members yet? Monica and the Irish couple?"

Sadowski shook her head. "With all that's been going on lately, I haven't had the chance. I'll get onto it this afternoon."

Granger nodded. "The two women can stay and defend the camp. We'll take the big fellow with us. He doesn't look the type that scares easily."

"So long as he listens properly and does exactly what he's told." Sadowski sighed. "What a motormouth. He never shuts up, does he?"

Olvan smiled. "Jonah takes a little getting used to, that's all."

"That's hard when you can barely understand a word he says," Rollins added with a chuckle. "But from what I saw the other day, I think he's a little scared of you, Mary. There was real fear in his eyes when you dressed him down that time."

"Good," Sadowski said, cracking a dry smile. "By the time I'm finished with him, he'll be absolutely terrified."

The men around the table laughed.

"Last thing," Rollins said. "Let's not forget, Mason will have his plans too. We need to remain extra vigilant at the camp. He could attack at any moment."

The four other council members reflected on his words soberly.

"You'd think he'd just pack up and leave wouldn't you?" Perter said finally. "I mean, there must be easier fights to pick around here than us."

"He's not the sort, Hank," Granger said firmly. "Mason relishes confrontation. You pick a fight with a man like that, it's to the bitter end."

Rollins nodded. "Agreed. We just have to make sure it's *his* bitter end, not ours."

CHAPTER 3

It took Mason a couple of hours of roaming Lake Ocoee's north shoreline to find the kind of people he was looking for: folk down on their luck and a little desperate. Prior to that, he'd checked out several other camps, but none had suited his purposes. They were either too large or not interested in his proposition, and the survivors had viewed him with open hostility. Not that it had intimidated Mason. Accompanied by five well-armed crew members, he wasn't afraid of a little confrontation. In fact, he relished it.

He passed the turn for Archville, then moments later steered his GMC Canyon off Highway 64 and down a forest service road. "I saw a campsite back at that bay we just passed," he commented to Doney, who was riding shotgun in the front passenger seat. "If I'm not mistaken, this trail ought to take us down to it."

Fifty yards from the lake shore, a rudimentary barrier of boulders and a felled tree blocked the road. Beyond it was a small clearing where a couple of two-man tents had been pitched beside a travel trailer and a Dodge pickup. There didn't seem to be a lot going on, and the setup was poor. One thing caught Mason's attention, however: a flat-bottomed skiff anchored fifteen feet from the lake shore.

He pulled up in front of the barricade and beeped his horn. Immediately, several men emerged from the trailer and tents and scattered in all directions, taking cover behind the trees. Mason counted five in total. All carried weapons of some description

From behind a nearby tree on his left, a man dressed in army-surplus camos stepped out, a semi-automatic rifle clutched in his grip. He was obviously the camp member assigned to guard duty.

The man pointed his rifle at Mason. "What do you want?" he yelled. "This here property is taken. Turn around and be on your way!"

"I'm not interested in your shitty property," Mason growled. "If I was, I wouldn't be honking my damned horn." He glanced in his rear view mirror to see that two of his men had their rifles trained on the man. The other two in the truck bed scanned the rest of the camp. "Point that rifle someplace else before my men riddle you with holes."

The man stared uncertainly at Mason a moment, then lowered his weapon.

"That's better. Now tell me, where are you guys from?"

"Nashville. We got to the Cohutta three days ago."

"Nashville, huh? Where the music never stops." Mason chuckled. "I'm guessing it's stopped now though, right?"

"It's stopped all right. Won't be coming back anytime soon, neither," the guard replied. "What exactly is it you want, mister?"

Mason stared past him. From behind the trees, his companions all watched Mason intently, weapons at the ready. "You can start by telling me who's in charge here."

"That'd be Nate," the guard said, pointing over to one of the men. "The guy in the blue shirt. Why?"

Mason opened his door and stepped out of the truck. "Because I'm done talking to you, that's why. Go fetch him."

The guard held Mason's gaze a moment, then jerked his head to one side. "Nate!" he called out. "This dude wants to talk to you. Watch out, he's a big mother, too."

A stocky man in a short-sleeved blue-checked shirt stepped out from behind a tree and headed toward the barricade, two companions in tow. Thirtyish, he was around five-ten and looked like he had neither shaved nor changed his clothes in a week. All three men looked tough, and carried semi-automatic rifles. AR-15s.

When he got to within twenty yards of the barricade, the man stopped, waving to his two companions to do likewise.

"Yeah, what do you want?" he asked, warily looking Mason's huge frame up and down. "From here on down to the lake is private property. We don't let no one pass through."

"So I heard," Mason replied. "You Nate, the leader of this group?"

"That's right."

"How many of you are camped here? Just the six of you?"

Nate eyed Mason suspiciously. "More than that. What the hell is it to you?"

"Because I got a proposition for the right sort of people who can help me out on a certain matter. Maybe a group looking to improve their situation." Mason glanced back at the shabby camp. "Which in your case wouldn't take much doing."

Nate scowled. "We were doing just fine until bandits ambushed us on our way from Nashville. I lost four men and was forced to hand over most of our supplies."

"These are tough times. Ambushers everywhere." Mason turned to face Doney, who by now had stepped out of his side of the vehicle, and winked. "That right, Doney?"

"That's right, boss. You got to be real careful how you go about these days."

Nate studied the two men. "How about you tell me your proposition. If I'm interested, I'll tell you how many men I got."

"Fair enough. I got a situation going down on the other side of the lake. A situation where I could do with a little help. For that, I'd be prepared to give away some of my supplies. I got medicine, fuel, dry foods, and a bunch of other stuff you could probably do with right now. In fact, if you did a good job for me, I might even allow you people to settle next to my camp. Trust me, no one is going to fuck with you if I'm anywhere nearby."

"Where exactly is this camp of yours?" Nate asked.

Mason pointed across the lake. "A place called Wasson Lodge. Over on the south side."

Nate frowned. "Just so happens we were there when we first arrived and got run off the place. Was that you guys?"

"Nope. We only moved in recently. The lodge is under new management now." Perhaps it had been Mason's men who'd chased Nate away that day. He had no idea.

"So what happened to the old management?" Nate asked, staring at Mason closely.

"I'll leave that to your imagination. Here's the thing though, I got a big group and the lodge is too small for me, so I'm planning on moving somewhere bigger."

"You're thinking of the YMCA camp, ain't you? It's on the same piece of headland."

Mason nodded.

"Thing is, it's currently occupied right now," Nate continued. "So you'll need to shift the management there too, won't you?"

Mason grinned. "You're a quick learner, Nate. Help me take it, and the lodge is yours." He indicated to the barricade. "How about you let me in and I'll tell you all about my plan. Play this smart, and by this time tomorrow you'll be living somewhere comfortable with new friends close by for safety. How does that grab you?"

Nate stared at Mason for several seconds. Then he turned to his two companions. "Joe, Matt, pull back the barrier and let them in. Ain't no harm in talking."

CHAPTER 4

At the north end of Camp Benton's headland, Mary Sadowski stood next to a short row of sandbags stacked eighteen inches high. Standing attentively in front of her, with their backs to the lake, were Jonah Murphy, his wife Colleen, and Monica Jeffreys.

Seventy-five yards away, close to where Russ had been executed that morning, were three wooden stands, each with an eight-inch cardboard square attached to them. Clipped to the squares were homemade paper targets with a series of concentric circles scrawled on them in thick black marker. In the middle of each, colored in red, were the targets' three-inch centers.

Mary was about to commence weapons training with the newcomers. By now, all three had been made aware of the emergency situation at the camp, and that it could come under attack at any time. Though they had been taken aback by the alarming turn of events, the three were part of the Benton group now, and had assured Mary they were committed to defending the camp.

"Right," she said, striding up and down in front of them like a drill sergeant. "Have any of you had weapons training before?"

Monica and Colleen shook their heads. Only Jonah raised his hand.

Typical, Mary thought to herself. *It had to be the motormouth.* She walked over and stood directly in front of him. "All right then. Where and when did you receive your training?"

"A few days ago," Jonah replied. "Outside a gun store on the Osceola Parkway, Orlando. Yeh probably don't know where that is, do yeh?"

"Nor do I care," Mary answered curtly. "And *who* exactly gave you this training?"

"Eh…Bill O'Shea and his buddy Darren." Jonah indicated to the Armalite M-15 rifle he held in front of him, its butt resting on the ground. "They taught me a cool firing stance for the rifle, and another for me Glock. When I got back to the hotel, I taught it all to Colleen." He looked at his wife reprovingly. "Yeh really should have raised yer hand too, love."

"Jonah, you hardly qualify as a weapons instructor," she replied firmly. "Which is precisely why I didn't raise my hand."

"My training helped you kill three skangers on our way here," Jonah protested. "If I hadn't—"

Mary shot up the palm of her hand directly in front of his face. "*Please.* Not another word." She turned to Colleen. "You really killed three people?" she asked curiously.

Colleen nodded. "Killed or severely injured. To be honest, Jonah's training was pretty good."

Jonah looked like he was about to say something more. Mary raised her hand again, giving him a stern look.

"Mary, I'm afraid I don't have any weapons," Monica said hesitantly. "I haven't had the opportunity to pick any up yet."

"Don't worry." Mary gestured toward the sandbags where two rifles rested against them. One was hers, the other a LaRue PredatAr AR-15-style rifle, a spoil of war taken from one of Mason's guards at Old Fort the other day. "I have a spare rifle for you to practice with. If you handle it well, it's yours."

"Thank you," Monica said nervously. "I fired a pistol once before, but never a rifle."

"You're going to do just fine," Mary reassured her. "All right, pay close attention everyone. We don't have much time, so we're going to pack a lot into this session."

She spent the next thirty minutes going through the basics, starting with a safety check of their rifles, where she showed them how to remove the magazine and determine whether a round was already in the chamber or not. After that, she demonstrated how to load and unload the thirty-round magazines all three were using. Then it was on to clearing magazine jams, misfeeds, and other functional issues.

Next, she demonstrated the three main shooting positions: standing, kneeling, and prone, showing how to use the environment to maximize firing stability. As one example, she grabbed the side of a nearby tree and rested the rifle in the V between her thumb and forefinger to get a stable shooting position that improved aiming and trigger control.

Finally, they got to the part she knew they were all waiting for: target practice. Using the sandbags as shooting rests, she taught them how to fire from the prone position, ensuring they understood the basic mechanics on how to squeeze off accurate rounds: legs spread apart, shoulders level, head upright, support arm at a ninety-degree angle.

Both Jonah and Colleen's shooting was impressive, and the two kept their shots in tight groupings. Monica was extremely nervous, however, and her shots went wild. Mary did her best to encourage her.

Swapping out the paper targets, she took the three to within fifty yards of the stands and demonstrated the best shooting technique while on the move, taking into account Ned Granger's recent comment to her that in all his years of combat, he'd rarely gotten the chance to shoot from the prone position.

She gestured for Colleen to come over to her. "All right, take a couple of steps and move into your shooting stance. Fire off three quick shots with the mag hold grip I showed you. I think it suits you best."

Colleen took three paces, then placed her left foot forward and raised the rifle up to her right shoulder so the iron sights were at eye level. She pushed her head down tight, hunched her shoulders, and with her left hand clutching the magazine for support, popped off three shots in rapid succession, mimicking the type of real life action she could expect.

Mary looked at her approvingly as she lowered the weapon. "Nice, smooth shooting. Run down and fetch your target. Let's see how you did."

A minute later, Mary inspected the paper target, noting with satisfaction the sub six-inch grouping around the center bullseye.

"Close enough for government work," she said. "Not that there's much of that around these days."

Monica stepped up to the line and fired off her three rounds using the same technique as Colleen. Her shots were far wider than Colleen's. Two rounds missed entirely, while one caught the very edge of the target.

"Needs improvement," Mary told her, "but not bad for your first attempt. Next time, fire off your shots a little slower until you get the hang of it." She wagged Jonah over with her finger.

Jonah strutted forward and raised his Armalite to his shoulder. Rather than gripping the magazine with his left hand, he extended it and grabbed the rifle's fore-end in a C-clamp grip, the one *Bill* had shown him back in Orlando. He squeezed off three shots in rapid succession.

Showoff, Mary thought to herself. Still, she had to admit the Irishman's posture and trigger action had been excellent.

"Go get it," she told him curtly. With a grin, Jonah sauntered down to the stand, returning a minute later with an even bigger smile as he handed her his target.

Mary stared down at it. All three rounds were tightly grouped around the bullseye, and one had even clipped the edge of it. She gave him a brief nod. "It's a relief to see you're more than just a bigmouth."

Standing three feet away, Jonah grinned. "I've always had a good eye. Used to do great with the old air rifle at the fairground. I was pretty good at the coconut shy too."

As he spoke, Mary caught a strong whiff of beer off his breath. A large frown broke across her face. "Jonah, have you been drinking?"

The Irishman took a step back. "Eh, no. Why do yeh say that?" he said, speaking out of the side of his mouth.

Mary snorted. "Because I smell it on your breath, that's why. Don't lie to me."

Jonah looked at her uneasily. "Well, now that yeh mention it, I might have had a beer or two after lunch. Helps with me digestion, don't yeh know."

Mary looked at him sternly. "I will not tolerate anyone handling firearms under the influence of alcohol."

"Mary, I wouldn't call it 'under the influence,'" Jonah protested. "Sure, a couple of tinnies doesn't even give me a buzz. It'd take a lot more—"

"*Jonah!*" Mary thundered. "You will not drink alcohol again until this issue with Mason is resolved. Our camp could come under attack at any moment." She turned to Colleen. "After we're done here, bring over all the alcohol in your cabin," she ordered her. "And I mean *all* of it."

Colleen glanced quickly at her husband, then nodded.

"Mary!" Jonah protested. "That's...that's not—"

"Yes, it is fair. And no, it's not stealing. You'll get it all back when the situation has normalized. Until then, all alcohol is prohibited here at the camp. Do I make myself understood?"

A clearly shell-shocked Jonah nodded his head forlornly, speechless for once.

"Good." Mary nodded. "All right, Colleen, you're up again. Let's see if you can improve on your last score."

***

"She's taking *all* me gargle?" Jonah said in a high-pitched yelp as he and Colleen walked back to their cabin an hour later. "That's not right. It's not like I'm a problem drinker or anything," he spluttered furiously.

"Well, it does run in your family," Colleen said quietly. "Your father has gout, and just look at what happened to your Uncle Paddy. Dead at fifty-three."

"Colleen, I'm not like Uncle Paddy!" Jonah protested. "He was on the whiskey before his first slice of toast in the morning." He paused a moment to reflect. "By *jaysus*, there was some drink taken on the day of his funeral, though. Do yeh remember love?"

"Yes, I remember. I'm surprised *you* remember anything of the day," Colleen said dryly.

They reached their cabin. "Now listen, Jonah," Colleen said as they walked up the porch steps, "I'm going to collect your beer and whiskey and take it over to Mary right now. And I mean *all* of it."

Jonah glowered at her. "Teacher's pet. Yeah, she loves *you* all right." He sighed. "Go on, take it. Guess I'll just have to suffer in silence, won't I? It won't help with me blood pressure, you know."

"What are you talking about? You don't have high blood pressure."

"Because a glass of whiskey in the evenings prevents it, that's why. Doctor McGillycuddy told me that on me last checkup. Just a sup, mind."

A smile came to Colleen's face. "How about we have a little afternoon fun when I get back? That helps with blood pressure too, they say."

Jonah's eyes lit up, instantly forgetting his woes. "How about the hot stuff, love? Will yeh put it on for me? Seeing as I hauled it all the way from Orlando, it'd be a shame for it to go to waste."

Colleen laughed. "Yes, Jonah. I'll put it on." She stepped into the cabin and looked around the room. "Now…where have you stashed all that drink of yours?"

CHAPTER 5

"I don't trust him, Nate. You sure we should go through with this?" Matt Cooper asked as soon as Mason and his crew departed. Cooper was Nate Gingell's second in command. From the very outset, he'd made it clear that he opposed Mason's proposal, and had listened in stony silence throughout the entire meeting.

Nate, on the other hand, didn't give a damn about the fact that he'd just agreed to oust another group from their camp. It was dog-eat-dog these days, way beyond the issue of morals.

He and his men had arrived in the Cohutta less than seventy-two hours ago, and had wandered up and down the lake's shoreline looking for a decent place to camp, getting yelled or shot at in the process.

Exhausted and demoralized, they had finally claimed a spot at Greasy Creek, an inlet just east of where Highway 30 ran north up to Archville. At the top of the inlet was a campground, already occupied by a group of fifteen. Luckily, Nate and his men had managed to set themselves up at a tiny bay on the west side. Tucked out of the way, the larger group hadn't objected to their presence.

Finding a boat had been their first priority. By now, all had been taken from the surrounding lakeside properties.

Heading up Highway 30, however, he and Matt had eventually spotted the sixteen-foot skiff on the front lawn of a house three miles south of Archville.

Busting into the garden shed, they had retrieved its fifteen horsepower motor. Also in the shed they found a half-full ten gallon gas can, and a smaller can of oil for the two-stroke engine. The boat was already mounted on its trailer, and in a matter of minutes the two had hitched it up to Nate's truck and driven it down to Greasy Creek.

"At least we'll be safer with Mason," he told Matt. "You really want us stay here and keep beating off the gangs?"

Though their camp was too small to interest the larger groups, there had been plenty of others keen to take their spot at the lake shore.

Matt stared at him doubtfully. "You really think Mason is just going to hand over the lodge to us? That's prime real estate."

"Why not? It suits both of us."

"Maybe he's looking at taking over our group. You ever think of that?"

Nate hadn't. The notion startled him for a moment.

"Because I for one wouldn't like that," Matt continued. "That guy is scary."

"Right now, *life* is scary. And in case you haven't figured it out, we're low on choices."

Matt sighed. "I guess so. By the way, what are you going to do about our three other *hunters?*"

During the meeting, Nate had lied to Mason about the size of their group, telling him he had another three men out hunting at that moment. He'd felt Mason mightn't be interested in any deal if he thought his group was too small for the task ahead.

He grinned. "They all get killed tonight storming the camp. That's okay. I never thought much of them anyway."

***

There was a curious look on Doney's face as Mason steered the Canyon back up the forest track toward the highway. "Boss, you really plan on giving Nate the lodge?"

Mason shrugged. "Why not? If they're good fighters, no harm in keeping them close by. Besides, it'll save us the hassle of having to defend it."

In return for Wasson Lodge and some provisions – courtesy of the lodge's previous occupants – Nate had agreed to contribute his men to the attack on Camp Benton that night. During the negotiations, he'd noted how quickly Nate had agreed to ally himself to him. It didn't surprise him. Competition was fierce at the lakeside, and a group their size would always struggle. He very much doubted whether Nate had several other men out hunting in the forest like he'd said.

He cast his mind back to a discussion he'd had with Russ the other day. The survival rate for vPox was around two percent. Many had barricaded themselves inside their homes to escape the disease. It meant that perhaps tens of thousands could be wandering around Tennessee. Russ had been confident, however, that over the course of the next few weeks that number would quickly dwindle. Food stocks had already run out, and most people had no idea how to hunt or fish. Those pushed to the marginal areas by the larger groups would soon die off.

Both had agreed that the key to survival was to control prime territory, something Mason was determined to do. It meant he needed to do everything in his power to make sure that tonight's attack on the YMCA camp succeeded.

They reached the highway. Mason swung right onto it, heading east in the direction of Archville.

Doney raised an eyebrow. "Where we going now?"

Mason grinned. "The day is still young. No reason why we can't find another group to help us out tonight. Wasson Lodge is a hell of a prize in return for a little muscle."

Doney stared at Mason. "So how you going to decide who gets the lodge? Nate or the next group we find?"

"Well now, that depends."

"On what?"

"On whoever fights the hardest."

A broad smile came over Doney's face. "I like the way you're thinking, Boss. Could be a fun night."

CHAPTER 6

As soon as Cody and Walter returned to Camp Eastwood, Walter convened a meeting during which he explained what had occurred at Camp Benton to the group. Though he mentioned his own involvement with Mason back in Knoxville, he was careful not to say anything about Pete's rash judgment that had initiated the connection with the bandit in the first place. Nonetheless, Cody could see how distressed Pete was to hear about the brutal murders at Wasson Lodge.

"D-Did no one other than Liz survive?" he asked haltingly.

"Perhaps Mark managed to escape," Walter replied. "Liz isn't sure."

"How come she didn't come back with you two? Doesn't she want to join us?"

Walter shook his head. "I gave her the option. Guess she feels safer at the Benton camp."

"From what you say, don't sound like this guy Mason cares too much for you, Walter," Ralph said. "That going to be a problem?"

"It could be. Back in Knoxville, Cody killed a couple of his men while he and Pete helped me get away from him."

"So what happens now?" Maya asked with a worried frown. "How's this thing going to play out?"

"I'm meeting Sheriff Rollins later today to discuss plans, so we'll know soon." Walter looked around the group. "Other than for myself, Pete, and Cody, this isn't really anybody else's fight. All the same, Mason is a merciless killer who has just murdered several good people. If anyone feels like volunteering to help get rid of him, it would be appreciated."

Ralph nodded his head. "Count me in."

"Me too," Clete followed. "Looks like we're involved in this whether we like it or not."

"Thank you," Walter said appreciatively. "The sheriff will be happy to know he has five more men at his disposal when he needs them." He glanced at Greta. "All right. Onto other matters. Now that there's fifteen of us, I think it's time for us to move down to the valley. We can't hide up here in the hills forever."

***

The move took all day. While the actual packing and hauling of trailers took no time at all, the setting up of the farm's defenses still weren't finished by sundown. By now, though, most of the group had experience in building fortifications and good progress was made.

Walter supervised the proceedings using the hard-won practical skills he'd learned from nearly twenty years in the military. He based his plans on OCOKA, the US military acronym that stood for: Observation; Cover and Concealment; Obstacles; Key Terrain and Avenues of Approach, and his detailed sketches integrated all five of these principles.

Cody, Clete, Simone, and Jenny began the arduous work of constructing the defensive perimeter using the materials brought back from Dalton City the other day. Before joining them, Ralph and Pete drove off to a neighboring farm they'd passed on their way back from their Georgia trip. Wearing thick gloves, they uprooted fence posts and razor wire, also some paddock fencing that Marcie had asked them to find, and hauled it all back in the utility trailer.

Within the perimeter, Walter, Greta, Emma, and Maya stacked sandbags around the farmhouse, building a guard post at each corner. On top of a tall barn, several more were hauled up to be used as cover for a sniper position.

Rocks, barbed wire, earth-packed flower beds, and felled trees from the previous camp were all carefully interwoven to prevent vehicles from simply bursting into the property, and positioned to funnel any would-be attackers into several ambush points around the property that Walter had meticulously designed.

Farm machinery, including a small combine harvester and a John Deere tractor, were driven into place to provide cover for the front and back of the farmhouse. On the east side of the property, the deep waters of the Connasauga River offered natural protection, and gunner positions were placed along its banks, ready to fire down upon anyone who tried to swim or row across.

The group continued to maintain a lookout posted at the top of a nearby hill, from where both entrances into the Alaculsy Valley could be observed. Being farther away than before, the change of guard was slower, but armed with two-way radios, the information relayed was still instantaneous. As before, guards were changed on four-hour shifts.

In charge of the farm work was Marcie, with young Billy second in command, the only two with "real" farming experience. Along with a begrudging Fred, a smiling Eric, and a chirpy Laura, the five set about the initial organization of the farm.

First, they inspected the main farmhouse, which thankfully had no dead bodies inside. Though by no means modern, and slightly rundown, the four-bedroom building suited their needs perfectly.

"Excellent," Marcie said to Simone with satisfaction. "Tonight, let's just pitch up our tents in that plot over there," she said pointing out the window to a large field on one side of the farmhouse. "I'll talk to Walter later about sleeping arrangements. Hopefully, he lets us and the children take these bedrooms. For the moment, we'll just give them a good clean out."

The house had a big kitchen and dining room. Outside, there was a large vegetable patch in the backyard. It had an herb garden too, where Marcie identified basil, oregano, rosemary, sage, and thyme.

The animals had all survived the trip from Gainesville. The chicken tractor was wheeled into the shade around the back of one of the work sheds, and a thirty-foot square area marked out that would be turned into a chicken pen. The rabbit hutches and nesting boxes were placed in another area, while the two goats, William and Betsy, were tethered on long ropes in an unused field where the grass grew high.

The ducks were brought into the far corner of the backyard, where a stand of poplars offered some shade. A large plastic container found in one of the work sheds was filled with water from the river, and the team got great pleasure watching the five ducks and the drake splash contentedly inside it. On the group's next scavenging run, Marcie intended on asking someone to source a plastic kiddie pool at a Kmart or a Target. That would suit them even better.

Finally, two plots were measured out in a field where the tunnel hoops would be erected in the coming days. Once the soil was tilled, seeds taken from Billy's farm would be planted. Later, they would prepare other areas of the property to grow vegetables, using the seeds Fred had brought with him from Maysville.

By sunset, Walter was satisfied with the day's work. "We've made a great start. Plenty more to do tomorrow, though." He clapped his hands. "Right, everybody.

Chowtime! Cody, start cutting steaks from that deer you bagged yesterday and get them on the grill. Nothing like honest hard work to build up an appetite!"

***

Other than for the three guards on evening watch, the group ate in the backyard where Fred, Simone, and Jenny worked the barbecue, which had been brought onto the patio in the herb garden. The patio was covered by a large trellis, and underneath it was a wooden table and six chairs. It looked to have been a popular spot for the family living there prior to the pandemic.

As well as delicious cuts of venison, potatoes and fava beans from Billy's farm were cooked in the kitchen on a gas stove, and to celebrate the move to their new camp, precious tins of peaches and apricots were opened for dessert and served with condensed milk.

The guards weren't forgotten either. A plate laden with food was taken out to Clete, who sat in the bucket seat of the combine harvester. A similarly-laden plate was served to Emma at the back of the house, who sat perched on a stack of sandbags on the flat side of the barn roof.

Simone had gotten the shift's remotest gig as main lookout at the top of the hill. Nonetheless, food packed by Marcie in plastic containers was delivered by Billy, and the two friends sat together a hundred and fifty feet above the camp, eating their dinner hungrily.

To the west, the sun had sunk behind the mountains, though it still shimmered along its crests. Below, the valley was covered in shadow. Though cooler, the night was warm and the two wore only T-shirts and shorts.

Simone pointed to the night vision binoculars at her feet, which Walter had given her for the watch. They were still packed away in their hard case. "Once it's dark, let's check out these NVGs." She grinned. "They're the best that money can buy. They cost over four thousand dollars."

Billy eyes lit up. "That'd be cool!" he said, chewing on a piece of venison. "Maybe we can test how far away you can spot me."

"Great idea. Walter told me that, depending on the ambient light, they can detect anything moving up to five hundred yards." Simone reflected a moment. "You know, Billy. I'm glad Pete managed to convince us all to come back with him." She stared down at their new camp. "I think we made the right decision, don't you?"

Back at Willow Spring, it had taken a lot of persuasion for the group of five to leave the farm. Simone and Marcie had been convinced first, then Eric, and finally an obstinate Fred and Billy. Seeing as it was the farm where he had been raised, Billy had been the most distraught. Nonetheless, once everyone else had decided on traveling to the Cohutta, he knew he couldn't face being alone again and had finally acquiesced.

He nodded. "I didn't want to at first, but now I'm glad I did. People here are nice."

"Yes, they are." Simone smiled and looked over at him. "This is our new home now."

***

After they finished eating, coffees in hand, Walter took Cody, Pete, Ralph, and Clete up to the end of the garden, where a wooden bench was positioned beneath a stand of poplars. A few feet away was the plastic container that served as the duck pond. There was no sign of the ducks.

"What's up?" Cody asked as he sat down beside him on the bench. Pete, Ralph, and Clete stood next to him.

"I talked to the sheriff a couple of hours ago," Walter told them. "The Bentons intend hitting the lodge tonight. No point in just waiting for Mason to attack them."

Clete nodded. "Makes sense. That way they can make better use of us."

"Exactly. Rollins wants to coordinate an attack from three different positions. The main force will come through the forest, another one will arrive by boat around the headland, and we'll come at them from the south via Devil's Point."

Ralph grunted. "Sounds like a plan. What time is kickoff?"

"Three a.m. I told the sheriff we'd be down there by two. That gives us plenty of time to coordinate everything." Walter looked around at the four men, a serious look on his face. "Get to bed early tonight. Try and get a couple of hours rest. I'll be around to wake you all up at 1 a.m. Have your weapons ready and bring plenty of ammunition. It's going to be a long night."

CHAPTER 7

At 12:30 a.m., Nate gathered his men. The seven strode down to the lake shore, rifles slung over their shoulders, jacket pockets and tactical pouches stuffed with extra magazines. One of the men waded out to the skiff, drew up the twelve-pound anchor, and stowed it in the front hatch. Lowering himself back into the water, he pulled the boat closer to shore and the men clambered on board.

Matt, the only member of the group with any nautical experience, started up the fifteen-horsepower motor and steered the boat out into deeper waters. When they reached the middle of the channel, only the pale moonlight to guide him, he turned west toward the Ocoee Dam. Though the night was warm, out on the lake the air was far chillier, and Nate was glad to be wearing a fleece jacket. With seven men on board, the skiff managed a steady twelve miles per hour as it chugged into a stiff headwind.

Twenty minutes later, they turned south and headed toward the Baker Creek Inlet, where the YMCA camp was located on its western shore.

A third of the way down, Cooper halved his speed, keeping the noise of the engine to a minimum. Though they were still over three miles to their destination, sound carried far over water. Cooper wasn't exactly sure how far, so he wasn't taking any chances.

On their left, the shadowy blur of the lake's eastern headland disappeared at the point where the mouth of the Indian Creek Inlet opened up. Cooper tugged the rudder and motored toward it. Once they reached the inlet, he steered the skiff toward the north shore, where a small wooden jetty protruded out into the waters. Twenty feet from it, he cut the engine and glided up to it, then expertly ran the dock line from a cleat on the boat to one of the pilings, and tied up.

Nate clambered onto the jetty. He checked his watch: 12:55 a.m. He pulled out the two-way handset Mason had given him earlier and keyed the radio. Three miles from Wasson Lodge and over open water, the radio would be within range.

"Mason, this is Nate. Do you read me, over?"

He had to wait several seconds for Mason's gruff voice to reply. *"Read you loud and clear. Wasn't sure if I'd hear from you again or not."*

"Never any question about it. Me and my men are at the Indian Creek jetty waiting for the go-ahead. Over."

There was a moment's pause before Mason spoke again. *"Await my orders and be ready to move in ten minutes. Over and out."*

***

At Wasson Lodge, a satisfied Mason tucked his radio back into the pocket of his combats. Combined with the gang he'd recruited after leaving Nate's camp, he felt confident he could take Camp Benton.

That afternoon he'd almost given up hope of finding more recruits when, around 4 p.m., he'd stumbled into a group of eleven men camped along a remote stretch of headland, accessible only by a forest logging road. The men looked like they'd been a rough lot long before vPox hit the streets, so much so that Mason and his team had almost tangled with them, and only some hasty communications between both parties averted a nasty firefight.

After a short talk lasting less than fifteen minutes, their leader, Don Gatto, agreed to join Mason's planned assault. Gatto had been a construction worker and was in his fifties. Broad shouldered, with shaggy gray hair and a harsh, rasping voice, it wasn't only the promise of the lodge that sounded good to him; he had a bone to pick with the Bentons too. He'd previously rumbled with them at their roadblock and had been forced to turn back. From his camp, Cookson Road was the most direct way for him and his men to reach the cities of Cleveland and Chattanooga, and he resented having to take the long way around each time.

Tania was sound asleep when Mason cinched his web belt, loaded with extra magazines in their Velcro pouches. Better that way. He neither expected nor wanted a goodbye kiss before he left for battle.

He slotted his Sig Sauer P226 into its holster, grabbed his Heckler and Koch MR556A1 rifle, and headed out the door.

His men were waiting for him outside, armed and ready. "All set?" he asked Doney, walking over to him.

His bodyguard nodded. "All set, Boss. Ready to rock and roll."

The plan was to split the crew into two groups, one led by him, the other by Doney, and attack the Benton camp through the forest to either side of the driveway. Mason had a particular strategy in mind for coordinating all aspects of the attack between his four teams.

He grinned. "Then what are we waiting for? Time to get this party started."

CHAPTER 8

Since taking over Walter's trailer, Greta had converted it into what looked more like a tactical medical facility than a recreational travel trailer. Other than for the bedroom, the rest of the space was exclusively dedicated for emergency medical treatment.

The rollover couch in the living room had a vinyl cover placed over it, and in the cabinet next to it were the patient assessment tools used to evaluate, visualize, and measure vital functions. They included a stethoscope, a thermometer, and a blood pressure cuff, along with a battery-powered fingertip pulse oximeter for measuring blood oxygen saturation levels.

On the overhead shelf space were the equipment and supplies to treat most battlefield injuries: trauma scissors and strap cutters for the removal of clothes and boots; 4x4 gauze to treat wounds; regular and hemostatic dressings of various sizes to dress wounds; a CAT tourniquet for hemorrhage control; and an assortment of heavy-duty tape, bandage wraps, and splints to patch people up.

Across the aisle, the kitchen pantry was stocked with all manner of airway/breathing apparatus, such as oral and nasal airways, pocket masks, a manual suction device, and several endotracheal intubation devices. There was also a chest decompression catheter for patients displaying tension pneumothorax symptoms, typically caused by lung lacerations and one of the leading causes of death from chest wounds.

On inspection of the trailer, Walter had approved wholeheartedly. It was vital to have such facilities at the camp, and the infirmary had already demonstrated its capabilities when the wounded men and women of Camp Benton had been treated the other night. Since vacating his trailer to room with Pete, Greta had most certainly put it to good use.

***

Dressed in just a T-shirt and panties, Greta lay in bed under a thin cotton sheet. She stared up at the ceiling, a worried expression on her face.

"I just don't see why we have to get involved in this feud with Mason. It's not our fight," she said. She turned on her side to lean on her elbow. "You know, it's not too late to contact the sheriff and tell him we want out. He won't like it, but we have to put Camp Eastwood's priorities first."

Lying beside her, dressed only in his boxer shorts, Walter shook his head. "This is something we go to do," he said. "We got the Bentons into this mess, now we have an obligation to get them out of it."

The look of concern on Greta's face grew. "Mason and his men are animals. People could get killed tonight. *You* might get killed tonight." She smiled weakly. "You know how much that would piss me off? I've only just gotten to know you…intimately, that is."

Walter grinned. "Since you lured me into your den under false pretenses, you mean?"

Since they'd first gotten to know each other at Wasson Lodge, the chemistry between the two had been slowly developing. Two nights ago, while they were still camped in the hills, Greta had invited Walter to the trailer to show him how she'd set up the medical facility.

Afterward, they'd sat outside at the table discussing their lives. The conversation had been good enough for Greta to bring out a bottle of white wine and two plastic tumblers. Before the bottle was finished, they'd brought it inside and headed into the bedroom.

After making love, Greta'd confessed she'd been attracted to Walter since the moment she met him. Walter likewise confessed a similar attraction, though he felt guilty about the matter. It was only a little over two weeks since he'd buried his wife and daughter. Though Walter wasn't one for making excuses, Greta learned he hadn't gotten on with his wife for quite some time. The two had openly discussed they might separate as soon as their daughter had completed high school and went off to college. vPox had come first, however, and their plans, along with the rest of the world, had been shot to hell.

"I'm serious, Walter," Greta said, her tone more urgent now. "Don't go taking any risks tonight. Let the Bentons do most of the fighting. Remember, you got young Cody to think of. From what you've told me, he's a little too fearless for his own good."

Walter nodded. "You're right, I'll need to watch him. Make sure he doesn't do anything reckless. Still, that fearless attitude got me and Pete out of a bad situation that time with Mason in Knoxville."

Greta's face clouded. "Damn Pete. This is all down to him. What on Earth was he thinking of joining Mason's gang like that?"

"Don't be too hard on him. He's a good man. Ever since that day, he's made amends. He always volunteers first for whatever needs to be done, no matter how dangerous." Walter smiled. "And he did a good job hauling our first batch of recruits here too, didn't he? Next time, if he can find people out of their teens, and under the age of seventy, that would be even better."

Greta moved closer and rested her head against Walter's shoulder. "Laura is such a doll, isn't she? And

Simone, Marcie, and Billy are great assets to the camp. They've made great headway fixing up the farm."

"Yep. Everybody is going to work out fine."

Walter checked his watch. From her angle, Greta could see it was 12:30 a.m. "You going to catch any sleep before you leave?"

Walter shook his head. "I'm too restless for that. How about you? You sleepy yet? I'll go back to my trailer if you want."

"Nope. I'm kinda restless too." Greta leaned over and dragged herself across Walter's torso, then kissed him on the lips. "I say we have a little more fun. So long as you promise me it won't be our last time together."

Walter draped his arm around the small of her back and pulled her in closer. "Don't you worry about that. This soldier knows how to take care of himself. I'll make damn sure to come back to you in one piece."

CHAPTER 9

Sheriff Rollins sat hunched over the table in his cabin studying Ned Granger's plan under the light of a kerosene lamp. The attack on Wasson Lodge would commence in two hours' time, and everybody at the camp was fully prepared, the teams assigned, their leaders scheduled to convene in the council room shortly.

The main force would hike through the forest, led by himself and Granger. Mary Sadowski would command a Quick Reaction Force of six people, ready to engage the enemy on instruction, while Kit Halpern and one other man would canoe around the headland and up the tiny inlet Halpern had found the other day. Their orders were to get as close to the lodge as possible and act as spotters. Ideally, they would shadow Mason and relay his orders real time, as well as radio in the positions of his men. From Devil's Point, Walter and his group of five would attack from the south.

It was an excellent plan, and Rollins had confidence it would succeed. Like Granger, he couldn't wait to chase Mason out of the area. If they could kill him in the process, that would be even better.

A burst of gunfire chattered from somewhere close by. It began intermittently, but quickly turned into a fierce barrage of semi-automatic rifle fire. Rollins jumped up from the table and was clipping on his holster when his radio crackled to life.

"*Bravo Base, we got intruders in the forest! Do you read me, over?*" a young man yelled. In his haste, he'd forgotten to signal his position.

Rollins grabbed the radio just as the hand-cranked siren Bert Olvan had picked up the other day sounded the camp alarm. "This is Bravo One. What position are you reporting from, over?" he asked as calmly as he could.

"*Aw...shit! Sorry Sheriff, this is Papa Five,*" came the reply over the din of the siren. Papa Five was Camp Benton's most southerly post on their perimeter, the one nearest to Wasson Lodge, and most vulnerable to attack.

There was another crackle on the radio. "*Bravo Base, this is Papa One. We got shooting over here too,*" said a calmer voice. "*So far, we're keeping them at bay, over.*"

Papa One was the perimeter's northerly post. It appeared Mason was attacking the camp at its two most extreme points. Whether this was a serious attack or he was just probing their defenses was impossible to tell. Rollins hoped it was the latter, and that their own plans needn't be delayed, or at least not for long.

"*Break—Break! All posts...this is Bravo Two,*" Ned Granger's terse voice came over the channel, signaling for all on the frequency to listen. "*Hold your positions along the line. Reinforcements are on their way. Over and out.*"

Rollins shoved his radio into the front pocket of his shorts just as the siren ended. He grabbed his rifle and hustled out of the cabin.

Outside, the men and women of Camp Benton were likewise rushing about. Though a little frenzied, he was heartened to see they all appeared to know where they were going, and were making their way to their assigned posts around the camp.

He jogged across the main square and over to the council room, the rally point where he and Granger had prearranged to meet if under attack. By that time, Mary

Sadowski would be on her way to Papa Three with her QRF unit, ready to reinforce whichever section of the perimeter required the most help. Henry Perter and one other man would patrol the North Beach shoreline, while Bert Olvan did likewise at South Beach, both on the lookout for any water-based assault.

Ned Granger had already arrived. Leaning on his cane, he had his radio up to his mouth, barking out orders. "I've dispatched extra men to Papa One and Five," Granger informed Rollins when he reached him outside the council room. "We've now got fifteen in total across the entire perimeter."

"Will that be enough?" Rollins asked anxiously.

"Should be. There's a guard at each post with NV glasses. They'll cut to ribbons anyone trying to break across. So far it doesn't look like Mason is trying to overrun our positions. No point in over-committing resources until we see what he's got planned."

Rollins nodded, thankful to have someone in command who'd been under fire before. Unlike him, whose heart was beating fast, the squat figure of Granger personified coolness under pressure. Rollins listened as Granger kept a string of rapid exchanges going with all seven posts around the camp.

Granger's radio came to life again. "*Bravo Base, this is Bravo Five,*" Henry Perter called out urgently over the airwaves. "*There's a motorboat coming in from the north. Looks like it'll reach us in three or four minutes. Do you read me, over?*"

"Roger that, Bravo Five. Hold firm. Support is on the way," Granger snapped back. Keeping his finger on the Talk button, he stayed in transmit mode. "Rambler One, head to North Beach on the double. A motorboat is due to land imminently. Do you read me, over?"

"*This is Rambler One. Roger that,*" Mary Sadowksi answered back breathlessly. Rollins could hear the sounds of footsteps tromping through the forest, and guessed her six-man squad was already on their way. The QRF's role was to listen carefully to what was going on during battle and anticipate his or Granger's commands. "*ETA five minutes. Over and out.*"

Granger glanced over at Rollins and gave him a satisfied nod. Sadowski's team had several sharpshooters, including Jonah and Colleen Murphy. At the range that afternoon, the two had shown superb marksmanship. Still, Rollins was worried. Their perimeter was under attack and a motorboat was due to arrive on their shoreline at any moment. That wasn't good.

***

The QRF squad jogged single-file down the forest trail, rifles clutched in both hands, muzzles pointing skyward. A few minutes ago, Mary Sadowski had given the order to turn back from their route to the Papa Five post and head double-quick to North Beach instead.

Jonah Murphy quickened his pace to run alongside Colleen. "I don't like the look of this," he panted. "Mason must have a lot of men if they can attack us on so many sides." Sticking close to Mary earlier, he'd listened in on the reports coming from the posts along the camp perimeter.

"Splitting up his men weakens his force," Colleen said tightly, short of breath too. "Question is, which team contains the bulk of his men? That's the one his main attack will come from."

"Unless all of his teams are strong," Jonah replied worriedly. "Maybe he found a bunch more skangers to help him out tonight."

"Since yesterday? I doubt it."

Jonah wasn't so sure. Still, there was no point in arguing about it. He'd learned that arguing with his wife rarely paid off for him. In the midst of battle, it made even less sense.

Halfway to the beach, the sixty-two-year-old Mary Sadowski began to falter. Carrying her AR-15 and extra magazines on either side of her tactical belt, Jonah was surprised the sprightly lady had led the charge even this far.

Ahead of them, the sharp *rat-a-tat-tat* of rifle fire opened up like a string of firecrackers. The boat had obviously come into range. Almost immediately, a more distant barrage of gunfire peppered back in reply.

Crack! Crack! Crack! Crack!

Jonah ran ahead of Colleen to the top of the line. "Mary, how about you let me go ahead?" he said, running alongside her. "Hank's going to need help as soon as possible."

"All right," Mary panted. "Take Colleen and Jim with you. The rest of the squad will be right behind."

Still jogging, Jonah hollered back down the line. "Hey, Jimbo! Up here, headerball. We're going to lead the charge!"

A moment later, Jim Wharton raced up the path. A little chubby, he was powerfully built and was the camp's top shooter.

Jonah, Colleen, and Jim sprinted up the path. A couple of minutes later, they reached the end of the forest and burst out onto the beach where Jonah and Colleen had done their target practice that morning. The moon and the stars were out, and the lake's stony shoreline was clearly illuminated.

By now, the shooting had stopped. There was no boat out on the water, nor any sign of Henry Perter.

Jonah scanned the shoreline looking for any sign of activity. "Where in the name of jaysus *is* everybody?" he muttered.

"Jonah...over here!" a loud whisper called out on his left. Jonah spotted a figure waving to him from behind the tree line. He ran over to it and immediately recognized the tall, angular figure of Henry Perter leaning against a tree. Squatting beside him was another Benton man, one Jonah wasn't familiar with. It was plain to see he was injured. His face was set in a grimace, and he held his left arm out at an awkward angle.

"Hank, where the hell did that boat get to?" Jonah asked as soon as he reached them. "You chase it away?"

Perter pointed to the far end of the bay. "It headed around the back of the point."

"How many on board?" Colleen asked, catching up.

"At least six. When Noel got hit we had to pull back. We were too exposed on the beach."

Noel nodded, his pale face glistening with sweat.

"They've probably landed by now," Perter continued. "I've radioed it in. Mary and the rest of the team are heading over there now."

At that moment, gunfire opened up in the direction Perter had just pointed in. His radio came to life, and all five could hear Mary Sadowski's tense voice over the airwaves. *"Rambler One to Base. Contact on North Beach. A group of six or more men. We got them pinned down, but we need support. There's only three of us holding them back."*

Jonah's heart leapt. By splitting up the group, Mary's group was now severely exposed. "Come on, Hank," he urged. "We got to move."

Perter turned to his companion. "Noel, are you in good enough shape to come with us?"

Noel stood up. "Still got my shooting arm," he replied. "I'm good to go."

They took off. Perter keyed his radio and pressed it to his mouth. "North Beach to Base. Got a group of five heading over to Mary now!"

Staying parallel to the tree line, the five jogged quickly north in the direction of the gunfire. Over on the far side of the camp, the shooting had intensified too. Things were heating up.

CHAPTER 10

Nate and his crew crept through the trees, trying to skirt around a group of defenders that had taken up position seventy yards ahead of them. In the pitch dark, he couldn't make them out, but could see the muzzle flashes from their rifles. Every time he darted from one tree to the next, bullets whizzed viciously around him with alarming accuracy.

A couple of minutes ago, Matt Cooper had landed the skiff at a tiny cove around the back of the bay. After scrambling ashore, a steep, rocky track had led them into the forest, where they'd scattered as soon as they came under fire.

"Dammit, they must have NVGs!" Nate called out to Cooper as both men took cover behind adjacent trees. "No way in hell could they have found us so quickly otherwise." He checked his watch. It was 1:45 a.m. Mason needed him to be in position on the north side of the camp at 2 a.m., in position to attack the camp's main square. Forced away from the bay they'd originally intended landing at, they were running late.

"Matt, we need to split the team up," he whispered urgently. "If we're not at the square in fifteen minutes, we can kiss goodbye to Mason handing us the lodge."

"I'll stay back with a couple of men and lay down some covering fire," Cooper whispered back. "You go ahead, see if you can bypass their position."

Thirty seconds later, a fierce volley of gunfire opened up from Cooper and the two remaining men. Darting from tree to tree, Nate and three others pulled back from their position, then swung off to the right and jogged quickly away.

Using the set of earbuds Mason had given him for his two-way radio that morning, he raised him on the channel. "Mason, this is Nate. We've landed on the north side of the headland. Heading inland through the forest."

"You come up against much resistance yet, over?"

"Some. We got pinned down as soon as we landed. I had to leave some of my men behind to deal with them, over."

"How many of you are heading to the square?"

"Seven," Nate lied. His response included the three phantoms who would unfortunately perish in the ensuing firefight.

"Good. Keep heading inland. Soon as you arrive at the square, contact me again. Over and out."

***

Things were going well for Mason. Though his own team had yet to break through Camp Benton's heavily defended perimeter, it was now under severe pressure. It helped that Nate's team had made contact on the north headland and drawn several defenders over in that direction.

He still had one more trick up his sleeve. Using the arrow keys on his handset, he changed over to Don Gatto's frequency and raised him on the channel. "Hey, Gatto, this is Mason. Where are you, over?"

A moment later, Gatto's rasping voice flooded into his head through the tiny earbuds. *"We're out on the lake. About a mile offshore and awaiting your signal. Sounds like you started the party without us. That's not cool."*

Mason chuckled. "Don't worry, there'll still be plenty of beer when you arrive. Matter of fact, why don't you come over now and join the fun?"

"*Roger that. On our way. Over and out.*"

Mason pulled out his earbuds and slipped the handset back into his pocket. He smiled grimly. So far, everything was going exactly to plan.

***

Shoulders almost touching, Jonah and Colleen raced through the forest with Henry Perter, Jim Wharton, and Noel following close behind. Around the camp, the shooting had intensified, and it appeared they were being attacked on all sides. Jonah could even hear sporadic gunfire as far down as South Beach.

Ten yards behind, Perter called out to him. "Jonah! Hold up a moment!"

Jonah and Colleen pulled up and waited for the three others to catch up. "Hurry up, guys!" Jonah said impatiently. "We need to get to Mary right away."

"Sure, but if she hears you crashing through the woods like that, she's liable to shoot you. We need to contact her first, let her know which way we're coming." Perter took out his radio again. "Rambler One, this is Bravo Five. What is your position, over?"

"*Bravo Five, this is Rambler One. We're on the southeast corner of the clear-cut. We got the intruders pinned down but need you right away. Where are you, over?*"

The location Mary referred to was a large clear-cut in the forest where the YMCA had recently started construction on some additional cabins. It was about three hundred yards from their current position.

"We're on the main forest trail. ETA to your position is three minutes. Over and out."

Taking off again, Jonah breathed a sigh of relief. It appeared that Mary and the rest of the QRF squad were holding their ground.

After jogging another fifty yards, Perter turned onto a secondary trail that would take them to the clear-cut. The five hiked up it single file.

Ahead, the shooting had died down and there was only intermittent fire. The same couldn't be said for the rest of the camp, however, and the reports coming over Perter's radio were becoming increasingly more ominous. Another boatful of attackers had landed somewhere along the south end of the peninsula. It explained the shooting Jonah had heard in that direction.

They arrived at the clear-cut where, behind the tree line, Mary and two others had taken up positions.

Jonah ran over to them and took cover behind a nearby tree. "Everything okay?" he called over to Mary.

"Yeah," she grunted, staring ahead without looking at him. Though the moonlight illuminated the deforested area of the clear-cut, it was impossible to see beyond the tree line. Mary gazed across at it, her night vision glasses raised to her eyes. There were only five sets of them, which Granger had distributed among the teams.

"Dammit," she cursed. "Looks like they split up. No wonder the shooting has thinned out." She raised her radio to her mouth. "Rambler One to Bravo Base, some of the intruders have slipped past our position. They may be heading in your direction. There's only two or three left here, over."

A moment later, Ned Granger replied. "*Copy that, Rambler One. Leave two men behind while the rest of you fall back to camp. They can follow you back, over.*"

"Roger that. Over and out." Mary called out, "Jonah, you and Noel stay here and hold the line. Give us five minutes, then follow us back. Got that?"

"Mary, Noel's left wrist has been shattered," Perter told her. "He needs medical attention right away."

"No, I'm good," Noel replied, though the look on his face indicated the pain he was in.

"It's okay, I'll stay behind with Jonah," Colleen volunteered.

"Colleen, you go back," Jonah said firmly. He knew that once behind the Ring, the camp's inner defense line, his wife would be safer than out in the forest. "I can manage these skangers on me own."

Mary stared at him briefly. "All right, but no heroics. Five minutes, then get back to the square."

"Don't worry, I'll be right behind yis."

Colleen squeezed Jonah's upper arm. "You hear that? No heroics," she whispered in his ear. "Or I'll murder you."

Jonah grinned. "I hear yeh loud and clear."

A moment later, the group of seven retreated from their position and headed back toward the main trail. Practically as soon as they'd left, Jonah realized just how vulnerable he was on his own in the forest. "*Jaypers*," he gulped, staring across the clear-cut and into the inky darkness. "That's another fine mess I've gotten meself into. What was I bleedin' thinking?"

CHAPTER 11

Rollins knew the tide had turned against them the moment Bert Olvan's breathless report came in over the radio. Olvan and a man called Ray Faber were the two on patrol at South Beach.

"*Bravo Four to Base. We got a boat coming in fast across the channel! Looks like it's going to land just north of us. Ray and I are on our way now to intercept it, over.*"

Rollins and Granger exchanged glances. "Copy that, Bravo Four. Report back as soon as you know the size of their force," Granger replied. While he remained calm and steadfast, Rollins knew his friend was under severe pressure. It looked like Mason had recruited *two* groups to help him with his assault on the camp. Not for the first time, Rollins cursed their luck that they hadn't scheduled their attack for earlier that evening, or this would be a very different scenario.

"Careful, Bert," Granger added, keeping his finger jammed on the Talk button. "I can't commit any resources to you yet."

It was becoming impossible for Rollins to keep up with what was going on, and for the first time in his life he came to truly appreciate the military term "fog of war." Mason was now attacking multiple points, with the last report indicating heavy gunfire at the Papa Two post. With Mary's

QRF squad only just returning from North Beach, he prayed the perimeter would hold. If it gave way, he knew all would be lost.

Granger turned to Rollins, his face creased with worry. "Mason must have recruited more than a dozen people. I'm not sure we can keep everyone at bay. We may need to give the order to retreat to the Ring."

Rollins felt dizzy. The Ring was their fallback position, only to be used in dire circumstances, just one step away from abandoning the camp. "Really? That bad?"

The grimace on Granger's face deepened. "We're not quite at that point, but it's close."

"All right, your call." Rollins glanced down at his watch. It was 1:53 a.m. Walter's group was due to arrive at Devil's Point at 2 a.m., in position to attack the lodge. Though that scenario was well and truly dusted, he could certainly put the additional men to good use.

He keyed his radio to the channel assigned to the Eastwood group. "Sheriff Rollins to Eastwood. Do you read me, over?"

There was no reply. Walter and his group must not have arrived yet and were still out of range. Through thick forest, radio contact was limited to under a couple of miles.

He tried again. "Rollins to Eastwood. We have an emergency situation. Do you read me, over?"

Still no answer. Rollins kept trying, praying that Walter arrived soon. It might make all the difference in saving Camp Benton.

***

Walter and his companions rode north along Baker Creek Road. Cody sat beside him in the Tundra's front passenger seat, while in the back of the crew cab were Ralph and Clete, their rifle stocks gripped between their knees. In the cargo bed, Pete sat on his own.

They had passed the Harris Branch ten minutes ago. Devil's Point was only five miles away, and the mood was tense. Mason ran a ruthless crew, vicious as scorpions, and the five knew that a dangerous night lay ahead, one that perhaps not all would survive.

"Almost there," Walter said, swinging the Tundra right at the junction with Card Spur, the road that would take them down to Devil's Point. "We should be in radio contact soon."

He pulled his radio out of his jacket pocket and tweaked the power button at the top of the device. There was the sound of static, and then a practically inaudible voice could be heard. "*Bravo...east...you...over?*" The message was too broken up to make it out properly.

"Not quite in range yet," Walter muttered.

"Why is he us calling us?" Cody asked. The attack on the lodge wasn't for another hour, and the plan had been that Walter would call the sheriff when the group arrived at Devil's Point.

"He's probably just checking we're on our way," Walter replied. "Maybe he's nervous whether we intend showing up or not."

Slowing down, he turned off Card Spur and onto a forest service road that would take them down to Devil's Point.

"*Rollins to Eastwood. Do you read me, over?*"

"This is Eastwood," Walter replied. "Read you loud and clear, Sheriff. Over."

"*Walter, change of plan!*" The sheriff's urgency could be heard perfectly now. "*Mason has attacked the camp. We need you to get over here right away. Over.*"

With a screech of the brakes, Walter pulled to a stop in the middle of the track. He turned to face Cody, both men's eyes widening. Mason and his crew had raided the Benton camp an hour before their own attack took place.

"Damn," Ralph said in the rear seat. "That royally fucks up our plan."

"Damn straight," Clete said, sitting beside him. "The fuck we do now?"

Walter raised the radio to his mouth again. "Roger that, Sheriff. How can we help, over?"

"Get back onto Cookson and park somewhere close to the camp driveway. We're under severe pressure along our perimeter. Can you do that?" Cody could clearly hear the sheriff's desperation.

"Affirmative," Walter replied. "Where do you need us, exactly?"

"On the right-hand side of the driveway, there's a trail that leads down to the south inlet. Our position is under heavy attack there. I'll radio them now and alert them you're coming. Over."

'Roger that, Sheriff. We're on our way. Over and out."

Walter put the pickup into reverse and turned it around on the track. "This is one badass firefight coming up," he said, worried, as he put the truck into forward gear again. "Let's hope we don't end up getting shot by both sides. Won't be the first time it's happened in my career."

CHAPTER 12

Jonah crept along the west side of the clear-cut, careful to keep out of sight behind the tree line. For the past few minutes, it had been eerily quiet, and he suspected the intruders had stolen away. Mary hadn't told him what to do in that situation, and his instinct was to go after them.

He reached the northwest corner. Holding his breath, he listened hard but heard nothing. He'd been right. The men had scarpered. To where, though? Only one thing made sense. They'd headed to the main camp to catch up with their companions.

A narrow footpath ran across the headland directly back to the square. The other day, Jonah had taken it on one of his walkabouts. Though riskier than heading through the woods, it would be the quickest way to catch up with the intruders. At a fast trot, he made his way along it, keeping as quiet as possible.

A few minutes later, he heard the sharp crack of a twig breaking under someone's foot ahead. It sounded nearby, and he halted. Perhaps the intruders were using the trail to guide them through the woods and were only a few feet to one side of it?

He stepped off the trail and crept in the direction where he'd heard the twig snap. Once off the path, it was even darker and he couldn't see more than a few feet. Just ahead, the crunch of a boot on the forest floor alerted him to how close the intruders were. He raised his M-15 to his shoulder, the selector already off safety.

Despite his bulky frame, Jonah was surprisingly light on his feet. With barely a sound, he continued quickly forward, and soon made out three shadowy figures ahead of him. Spread a few feet apart, they moved slowly between the trees.

Jonah aimed his rifle at the man on the left, took a deep breath, and squeezed the trigger twice in rapid succession. The man stumbled and fell to the ground.

"Jesus!" the fellow next to him screamed. Jonah swiveled his rifle toward him and popped off another couple of shots, then darted behind a tree as the man fired back.

"Matt! Where did he go?" one of them shouted.

"He's over there behind those trees," a wary voice hissed back. "Just one person, I think." Neither man sounded injured, which meant Jonah's last two shots had missed their mark.

He presumed that Matt had pointed toward the tree he hid behind. The muzzle flash from his rifle would have given him away. At that moment, several shots fired in his direction, whining past his ear. Yep, they knew his position, all right.

There was the familiar sound of a magazine being ejected. Jonah took that moment to dart away to his right, running as fast as he could. He tore through the trees, pine needles scraping his face and arms.

One of the men cursed, then commenced shooting again. Jonah heard bullets thudding into the trees around him, and the sound of bark splintering. Thirty yards later, he pulled up behind another tree, gasping for air.

He stopped for only a moment. In a low crouch, he crept through the forest in a semicircular movement, using the last muzzle flash he'd seen to gauge the intruders' position.

Until now, he felt he hadn't done much to contribute to the camp's defense. The last few minutes had changed that. He wasn't done yet, either. He was going to take out the remaining two skangers or die trying. Pushing Colleen's parting words *not be a hero* out of his mind, he continued as quietly as possible across the forest floor.

Whoever the remaining two men were, like himself, they obviously hadn't much in the way of combat experience. Unlike Jonah, however, they didn't have much in the way of street smarts, and he could hear them whispering long before he saw them. They obviously presumed he'd fled the area.

This time, he approached their position head on. Gauging the direction in which they were coming, he stepped behind a tree and held his breath. Seconds later he stepped out again. With his left hand C-clamped over the M-15's fore-end, he squeezed the trigger twice at the man on his right.

Crack! Crack!

He aimed at his companion, and unleashed two more shots. With no more than a single grunt between them, both men collapsed to the forest floor.

Jonah stepped forward, pointing his rifle down warily. Neither man stirred. Nonetheless, he pulled the trigger twice more, dispatching a bullet into each man's head, then headed back toward the camp, anxious to get back to Colleen.

War was a crazy thing. He'd killed three skangers and hadn't seen a single one of their faces. He'd get a rise out of Mary later, though. During training, the old battle ax hadn't approved of his fancy way of holding his rifle.

Even thinking about what had just transpired made him queasy, however. Some wise geezer once said that war was hell. He was dead bleedin' right. Killing three men in cold blood like that didn't make him feel good. Not one tiny bit.

CHAPTER 13

Mason and his team of six crept single-file through the forest, leaving two men behind to draw fire from the Benton defenders. After much probing, he'd found what he considered the best spot to squeeze past two perimeter posts and attack Camp Benton's positions from behind. Farther north, Doney and his men were in the process of employing a similar strategy. With the camp's defenses spread so thinly, especially now that both Nate's and Gatto's men had landed, Mason felt confident in his plan.

He kept off the forest trails, letting his excellent sense of direction guide him. From both left and right, the crackle of gunfire continued unrelentingly. In the dark, Mason grinned to himself. These were the moments he lived for: adventure, blood, and the satisfaction of improving his lot even further.

He and his team passed through the perimeter unimpeded. He swung left, and headed for the camp's main post on the driveway. After a short hike, through the gloom he could make out muzzle flashes from behind the big eight-wheeler parked across the road.

He took out his radio and contacted his second in command. "Doney, we've broken through their lines. I'm just south of the main post. Where are you?" he whispered.

"I'm through too, boss. I'll reach the driveway soon. We took some heat, though. Someone must have NVGs because they pegged two of my men, over."

Mason frowned, thinking hard. If the Bentons had people with night vision glasses, attacking the main post from behind made even more sense. "Don't think anyone has them around here. Nobody's spotted us yet. All right, I'll be in position in a couple of minutes. Wait until my signal. Over and out."

The plan was for Mason and Doney's teams to get behind either side of the eight-wheeler truck. That way they wouldn't risk firing at each other. Once they took out the post, both teams would head through the forest up to the main camp, leaving the isolated pockets of Benton defenders behind to be mopped up by his remaining men. With Nate's and Gatto's men closing in from each side of the headland, it wouldn't be long before he took the camp. Mason could feel it in his guts.

***

At the square, heavy gunfire opened up from the south. Bullets thudded into the backs of the cabins close to where Rollins and Granger stood, shattering windows. This was the first time the square itself had come under fire.

Minutes earlier, Bert Olvan had issued a garbled warning that the boat landing at South Beach had been packed with ten or more men. He and Ray Faber hadn't been able to hold them back, and had retreated under heavy fire. The attackers had chased them into the forest, and Olvan's last radio message had been to inform base he was turning his radio off so as to not give his position away.

Northeast of the square, a barrage of fierce gunfire opened up. The landing party that had eluded Mary's QRF squad had obviously gotten into position too.

Ned Granger had barely given the order to dispatch defenders along the fortified positions of the Ring when a frantic message came from Papa Three. Caught off guard and attacked from behind, the main perimeter had fallen.

Rollins had just returned to the square after supervising the defenses up at the parking lot.

"John, I'm calling it," Ned told him. "We've got to evacuate the camp."

Rollins stared at him numbly. His mouth went dry, and he could barely get the words out. "Okay, let's start getting people down to South Beach." Even as he said the words, he recognized the problem. The extraction route to South Beach was currently blocked by the newly-arrived landing party.

Granger was one step ahead of him, already on the radio to Mary Sadowski, instructing her to disengage from her current position and make a flanking maneuver against the South Beach attackers. As he spoke, further reports came in over Rollins's radio, describing how the bulk of Mason's force was now streaming in through the forest toward them.

Granger ordered everyone to retreat to the Ring and sent reinforcements to bolster the QRF's assault on the South Beach attackers. "John, we got to make an orderly retreat. If Mary succeeds, we need people to hold Mason back while everyone evacuates to South Beach."

"I'll stay behind and supervise," Rollins told him. "You get everyone away safely." He could barely believe he was saying the words. Their defenses had crumbled against Mason's ruthless, well-planned aggression, and the men and women of Camp Benton were running around in disarray, many in blind panic. How Mason had found extra men so quickly he had no idea, but there had to be close to forty in this highly-coordinated attack.

He raced across the square and returned to the parking lot where Mason would be arriving any moment, issuing orders on his radio to assemble more defenders there. At that moment, he remembered Walter. Things had moved so swiftly, he'd barely time to take him into consideration. He changed the frequency on his radio and hailed him.

"Eastwood, do you read me? This is Sheriff Rollins. What is your position, over?"

A moment later, Walter's calm voice came over the channel. *"We're at the south perimeter. We took out a couple of Mason's men, but it looks like your post has been abandoned, over."*

"The perimeter has been overrun. We can't hold the camp any longer. We're retreating to South Beach and evacuating by boat. Retreat from your position, there's nothing you can do."

There was a long pause, then. *"Shit. There must be something we can do to help. Over."*

Rollins thought hard. With all that had been going on at the camp these past few days, the Bentons had not yet organized any vehicles or provisions along Route 302, at the area where the evacuating boats would land, as had been their original plan. Once arriving at the end of the Baker Creek Inlet, the fleeing survivors would be stranded.

"Can you return to your camp and bring back vehicles to help with the evacuation, over?"

"Of course. We can be back in just over an hour. Where do you want to rendezvous?"

Rollins hesitated. He didn't want to risk giving the location where his survivors would land in case Mason had somehow cracked their privacy code. "Remember where Cody told me he bagged his first deer? My team will make our way there. Do you copy?"

It was a long hike from the southern tip of the Baker Creek Inlet to the Harris Branch. His group would arrive exhausted and demoralized. Still, he couldn't take the risk of Mason knowing their rendezvous point. That would spell utter disaster.

"Roger that, Sheriff. We'll be waiting for you. Over and out."

***

Crouched behind a large pine tree, Walter shoved his radio back in his pocket. Yards away, two of Mason's men lay dead on the forest floor. Fifteen minutes earlier, Walter had parked the Tundra on Cookson Road, hiding it between a gap in the tree line thirty yards before the entrance to the Benton camp. From there, the five men had jogged through the forest to the camp's southern post, where they had soundlessly moved in on Mason's men and clinically dispatched them.

He crept over to where Cody and Pete had taken position behind a nearby tree. Ten yards away, Ralph and Clete had done likewise, and he ushered them over.

"Listen up, Mason's taken the camp," Walter told the four once Ralph and Clete arrived.

Cody and Pete stared at him, aghast.

"You serious?" Pete finally uttered. "I can't believe it."

"Believe it," Walter said grimly.

"So what now?" Ralph asked, his tall figure crouching next to him.

"We need to get back to Eastwood and return with vehicles to evacuate them. Looks like Eastwood is going to be a refugee camp for a while."

***

At South Beach, the scene was frantic as men, women, and children clambered into the waiting skiffs. As soon as one filled up, its captain pulled back on the throttle of its outboard motor and headed full speed into the bay.

Earlier, at gunner posts along the fallback route, Rollins and his team had fought alongside Mary Sadowski's QRF squad, desperately keeping Mason's men pinned back until the last of the evacuees had passed along the extraction route. Then the two teams retreated from one defensive position to the next until they reached South Beach, and took up positions behind a line of sandbags at the very tip. Their final line of defense.

Soon all the boats had left, bar one. Only Rollins, Mary, Colleen, and three other Benton men remained on shore. Colleen had point blank refused to leave, hoping in vain for her husband Jonah to show up. Since he didn't have a radio, it was impossible to know what had happened to him.

So far there had been seven confirmed deaths, and Bert Olvan, Ray Faber, and Jonah were missing. Since going into radio silence, there had been no word from Olvan.

Crouched behind a sandbag parapet, Rollins keyed the radio one more time and tried to contact him. "Bravo Four, this is Bravo One. Bert, do you read me over?" Yet again, there was no answer. Finally, with the gunfire intensifying, Rollins grasped Colleen firmly by the shoulders and in a low crouch, the two sprinted over to the last remaining skiff where a Benton man had already started the engine.

Reaching the boat, Colleen broke free from Rollins grip. She spun around and shouted out, "*Jooonah!* Where are you!"

"Colleen!" Rollins yelled, spinning her back around. "Jonah isn't going to make it here. The place is swarming with Mason's men. He's probably hiding somewhere." He grabbed her arm and herded her toward the boat.

"He better be," Colleen said tearfully as she stepped into it.

Rollins, Mary, and the last two men jumped in, and the skiff, selected to leave last because of its powerful fifty horsepower motor, roared out into the bay. All five passengers laid down cover fire as Mason's men emerged from the forest and rushed down to the jetty, firing on the fleeing vessel.

The shooting soon dissipated as the skiff skimmed across the lake's glassy surface and headed out of range. Rollins took one last look to see torchlights crisscrossing South Beach, and Mason's men fired their rifles jubilantly into the air. He turned away, sick to the stomach. They had lost Camp Benton.

CHAPTER 14

Over on the north side of the headland, Jonah trudged through the forest. By now, other than for some sporadic shooting, the gunfire had stopped and he could hear whoops of celebration coming from the direction of the main camp. He smiled. The intruders had been chased away with their tails between their legs. What had they been thinking? The camp was too well-defended to be taken over by a bunch of mangy skangers. Sure, hadn't he just taken out three of them himself?

He reached the main trail and quickened his pace, fervently praying that Colleen was unharmed. He just wished he had a radio so that he could let her know that he was all right.

He emerged from the forest and out onto open ground. A hundred and fifty yards away, kerosene lamps flickered in the windows of the cabins around the square. When he got to within seventy yards, he slowed down. Between the cabins, he could see that a bonfire had been lit in the center of the square. People swarmed around it, some firing their weapons in the air, others laughing and high fiving. Something about the swagger of the men didn't seem right. He certainly couldn't imagine the likes of Sheriff Rollins or Ned Granger firing their weapons off like that.

He halted uncertainly in his tracks, and was about to dart into the cover of the forest when a group of three men emerged from out of the shadows and marched quickly toward him. It was too late to hide now.

When they reached him, Jonah didn't recognize a single face. His heart sank. "Oh my good *jaysus*," he muttered under his breath.

A burly, tough-looking man with shoulder-length gray hair stopped in front of him, his two companions on either side. "You one of Matt's men?" the man asked in a harsh, grating voice.

"Eh…yeah," Jonah replied, his mind reeling as he struggled to come to terms with the situation. Matt had been the name one of the men he'd killed back in the forest. It made sense to go along with the misapprehension for the moment.

The man nodded. "Nate told me three of you had to stay back in the forest." He looked behind Jonah. "So where is he? And the other fellow?"

"They got clipped in the forest. I'm the only one to make it."

The man glanced at his companions. "Aw, that's too bad. Lost a couple of good men myself." He stuck out his hand. "Don Gatto is my name. People just call me Gatto. How about you?"

Jonah clasped his hand. "Jonah Murphy. Please to meet yeh, Gatto."

Gatto stared at him quizzically. "That's a hell of an accent you got there, Murph. You're a long way from home, ain't you?"

"Yep, long story." Jonah glanced over at the camp. "What happened to the Bentons? They at the square?"

"Nah, we killed a few, the rest managed to escape by boat."

A sense of relief flooded Jonah's body. He prayed that Colleen had been among those who fled. "So most of them got away?" he asked as casually as he could.

"Yeah, they had an escape route that runs all the way down to the south bay." Gatto grinned. "If it had been me, I'd have burned all the boats and made my men fight to the very last man. This camp is a helluva prize."

Jonah forced a weak smile. "Bunch of yellow bellies. No wonder we took it so easy."

Gatto stepped forward and grabbed him by the arm. "Come on, Murph. Let's go find Nate. He'll be happy to see you. Then we celebrate. Mason just brought a bunch of beer crates down from the lodge. Whiskey too, I hear."

Jonah looked at him in alarm. He needed to avoid this Nate guy at all costs, or his cover would be blown. "Eh, how about we grab a beer ourselves first? Nate can wait a little longer." From the square, maybe he could slink off into the forest and make good his escape.

Gatto chuckled. "I can see where your priorities lie. Typical Irishman." He put his arm around Jonah's shoulder and ushered him toward the camp. "No, we better let Nate know you're okay first. I'm sure he's worried about you." He winked at his men, a sly expression on his face. One that made Jonah uneasy.

He and his three new companions walked through a gap in the line of sandbags that made up the Ring's defensive fortifications, then headed down one of the narrow footpaths between the cabins and entered the square. Mason's men stood around the bonfire with bottles of beer in their hands. Jonah counted nine or ten men, and presumed more would join soon.

Gatto nudged him in the ribs and pointed forward. "This way. Nate's up at the car park."

"Really…right now?"

"Yeah, Murph. Now," Gatto grabbed Jonah's arm tightly and led him across the square. Glancing behind him, Jonah saw that his men followed close behind. It didn't look like there was any way out of this.

He thought hard. Parked in the graveled lot was his Nissan. He had the keys in his pocket. Perhaps on the way, he could take out Gatto and his two friends. He might have to kill this Nate too. With the element of surprise though, he might get away in his truck and escape down the driveway.

The four walked around the southwest corner of the square. Instead of heading to the lot though, Gatto ushered him over toward the forest. Glancing behind him, Jonah saw that Gatto's men had drawn their pistols. Both were trained on him.

With a gut-wrenching sense of alarm, he knew he'd been rumbled. Gatto had been playing with him all this time.

"Ah now, w-what's all this about?" he stuttered.

"Easy there, Murph," Gatto said in a grating whisper, the menace in his tone plain to hear. "Nate is waiting. Come on."

They reached the edge of the forest. Gatto stopped and pointed ahead. "See? There he is."

Jonah peered into the forest but couldn't see a thing.

Gatto chuckled. "Murph, look down."

On the forest floor, ten yards away, Jonah made out four bodies lying sprawled on the ground. They were all very, very dead.

He spun around, his eyes widening. "Look, Gatto—"

Gatto waved a hand, cutting him off. "As you can see, it'll be me and my group taking over the lodge, not Nate. Listen to me good, Murph. I like your style, so I'm going to give you two options."

Jonah stared at him. "Yeah, headerball. Like what bleedin' options?" Gatto was fucking with him, and he was determined not to show any fear. He wouldn't give him the satisfaction.

Gatto looked at him appreciatively. "Option one. Join Nate and his crew." He grinned wickedly at Jonah. "Not much future in that."

"No kidding."

"Option two, you can join me and my crew. You look like the kind of guy I could use. What do you say?"

Jonah glanced down at the slain figures in the grass. "Besides the fact I barely knew the geezer, I'd be a fool to join a dead man, now wouldn't I? Yeah, Gatto. I'd be over the moon to join you and yer crew. Yeh won't regret it either."

Gatto's smile broadened even farther. "Who says personality don't count for nothing in these times? It just stopped you getting offed." He grabbed Jonah roughly around the neck and swung him around in the direction of the camp. "Come on, Murph. Let's you and me go get a beer, or even two or three. It's not like we don't deserve it. In fact, I say we party all night!"

"I'm game for that," Jonah blurted hoarsely. "Yer a sound man, Gat. I'll say that for yeh!" Weak-kneed, he staggered forward, walking lockstep with Gatto. One thing his newfound friend was right about. He badly needed a drink.

CHAPTER 15

At Eastwood, the mood in the camp was somber. Thirty minutes ago, the surviving members of the Benton group had been rescued at the Harris Branch in four pickup trucks and transported to the Alaculsy Valley. They were taken to the farmhouse, where the children were brought to bed, many still sobbing. Downstairs, the men and women sat around the living room with shell-shocked looks on their faces, devastated by the loss of their camp.

On his return, Walter posted extra guards around the camp perimeter, in case Mason somehow got wind of their location. While unlikely, given the events of the past week he was taking no chances.

After making his rounds, he entered the farmhouse and walked down the hall. Inside the kitchen, he found Sheriff Rollins, Ned Granger, Mary Sadowski, and Henry Perter sitting around the table, deep in conversation.

"Where's Bert?" he asked, coming over to the table. In the confusion of the past few hours, he'd yet to receive a full update on the night's events. "Didn't he make it?"

"We lost radio contact with him on South Beach," Rollins replied. "Hopefully, he managed to get away through the forest."

"I hope so. Bert's a good man." Walter hesitated before broaching the next subject. "How many did you lose tonight, Sheriff?"

"Seven dead, three missing, including Bert."

Across the table from Rollins, Mary Sadowski's face contorted with rage. "This is all your doing, Walter. If you hadn't brought Mason to the Cohutta, none of this would have happened."

It was hard to argue with that logic. "I'm sorry, Mary. We had no idea—"

She stood up abruptly, knocking her chair to the ground. "I don't care whether you meant to or not," she snarled. "You brought him here all the same. Thanks to you, we got seven dead, three missing, and twenty-four homeless people. I told you, John. We should never have let these people stay at the lodge. They've been nothing but trouble."

Before anyone could reply, Mary marched out of the kitchen and down the hall. Moments later, the front door slammed closed after her.

"I'm sorry, Walter," Granger said quietly. "She's upset, that's all."

Walter shook his head. "No need to apologize, I can't blame her for how she feels. In the meantime, until we figure this out, your group is welcome to stay here as long as you like. You have my word on that."

"Thank you. One thing I can tell you is we're not going to just sit around and cry. We're already making plans on how to take back the camp." Granger stared Walter firmly in the eye. "When we're ready, we'll be expecting your help."

Walter nodded. "When the time comes, everyone at Camp Eastwood will be involved. We're all in this together now. How big is his group? You say he recruited more men?"

Granger scrunched up his face and did a quick calculation. "Hard to tell. We killed five or six of his men. Perhaps thirty or so."

"Well there's over forty of us here now. So long as we remain vigilant, he won't take this camp."

"That's what I thought too, until tonight. I felt sure our defenses would hold." Granger shook his head bitterly. "I should have done better."

Rollins patted his friend on the shoulder. "Don't beat yourself up. Mason and his men are brutal, cold-hearted killers. That's hard to defend against. Thank God you prepared a well-designed escape route, or it could have been a lot worse." He pointed to Mary's overturned chair. "Walter, why don't you sit down and help us plan on how to retake Camp Benton. Like Ned says, we're not going to just sit around and cry. We may be down but we're by no means out."

CHAPTER 16

It had been two hours since Jonah had been almost "offed" by Don Gatto. Arriving back at the square, his first priority had been alcohol, and he'd gratefully gulped down two beers in quick succession to calm his nerves. A bottle of Jim Beam was doing the rounds and he'd taken a slug from that too. The alcohol did its job, and a more relaxed Jonah quickly ingratiated himself with his newfound friends while he figured things out.

He soon learned that Mason had sanctioned the hit on Nate. Mason had promised Wasson Lodge to two separate gangs and told Gatto that he was his preferred choice to move in. So Gatto had disposed of the competition, "to save any bad blood between us," as he had put it.

"Join Gatto or take a permanent nap in the woods. Some choice," one of Gatto's crew, a man by the name of Paul Webb, muttered sarcastically as the two stood drinking Coors.

As skangers went, Webb wasn't such a bad bloke. He was certainly far less unsettling than the bloodthirsty Gatto, and had confided in Jonah that he'd never been in favor of invading the camp in the first place. Once Gatto had made the decision, however, Webb's only option had been to join in or wander the lakeside on his own. Choices were tough in these times.

Beer in hand, the two stood at the northeast corner of the square. Over on the far side, Gatto and Mason talked animatedly. Other than for being introduced to Mason briefly, Jonah had stayed well away from him. The huge bandit exuded a dark menace that he was anxious to stay clear of. While Gatto was bad enough, Mason was your worst nightmare. Thankfully, Webb felt the same and the two had discreetly moved away from the gang leaders so they could talk more freely.

As they chatted, Jonah racked his brains trying to figure out how he could possibly find Colleen and the remaining Benton survivors. He knew that the fleeing boats had headed south down the Baker Creek Inlet, but had no idea where they'd landed, nor where the group had gone from there.

Though risky, his best bet would be to drive out of the camp. At least, that way, he stood a chance of finding them. On foot it would be close to impossible. Now that he was part of Mason's gang, he felt comfortable he could bullshit his way past any checkpoint. After all, he'd be leaving the camp, not breaking into it.

He checked his urge to leave right away, though. It was too soon to make his break. He needed to wait a few hours when he wouldn't be missed. In the meantime, he continued to do what he did best. Drink.

Breaking off in mid-sentence, Webb stared over Jonah's shoulder. "Hey, what's going on over there? Something's up."

Jonah gazed across the square where the crowd had started to whoop and holler as a group of three men made their way to the bonfire at the center.

Webb nudged him. "Come on, Murph. Let's check it out."

The two headed over. Peering ahead, Jonah checked out the new arrivals. They consisted of two of Mason's men, who held a third man roughly by each arm. His hair was disheveled and his face was bruised and bloody. As he drew closer, Jonah saw that the man was Ray Faber. He'd been on patrol with Bert Olvan that evening.

"Look what we found hiding in the woods, whimpering like a pussy!" one of his captors, a large barrel-chested man wearing a short-sleeved camo shirt, yelled triumphantly. "Looks like he missed the last boat out of here!"

A roar of laughter went around the crowd. "Should have bought his ticket earlier!" someone shouted back.

"Maybe he didn't have his fare and they chucked him off!" another yelled.

The man pushed Faber roughly forward. "Hey, Mason!" he hollered out. "What do you want to do with this one?"

Mason stepped away from Gatto. Obviously drunk, he swaggered forward, clutching a bottle of whiskey by his side. He reached Faber and stared at him coldly. "Your sheriff killed my man Russ," he said. "Put a fucking sack over his head and executed his ass. What you got to say about that?"

Visibly shaking, Faber stared at the huge gang leader. "I…I…uh…" he trailed off when he caught sight of Jonah standing twenty feet away. Jonah's heart beat fast. There was nothing he could do for Faber. He just prayed the frightened man didn't give him away.

"Hey, look at me!" Mason snarled. "I said, what you got to say about that?"

"N-Nothing," Faber stuttered, cowering in front of Mason.

The bandit's face contorted into a scowl. "Nothing?" he roared. "I'll teach you not to answer me!"

He stepped forward and grabbed Faber under each armpit, then dragged him in the direction of the bonfire. With a powerful twist of his hips, he flung him into the pile of blazing logs where, stumbling, Faber fell onto his hands and knees. With a howl, he jumped to his feet and stepped out of the bonfire.

With surprising speed, Mason pounced on him and threw him into it again. Each attempt Faber made to get out, Mason grabbed him and pushed him back in.

It was sickening to watch. "Poor bastard," Webb whispered to Jonah. "Can't someone put him out of his misery?"

On his next attempt to get out, a screaming Faber, whose clothes were now alight, ran desperately through the fire and out the other side, where Mason's men began to push him around, jeering at him.

Over on the far side, the gigantic figure of Mason ran toward the bonfire, his arms raised high above his head. He leapt into the air, and in what appeared slow motion, bounded through the flames and out the other side.

Aghast, Jonah watched as he strode over to Faber, who by now had sunk to his knees, trembling uncontrollably. Mason withdrew his pistol from his holster. Towering over Faber like an executioner, he pointed it down at Faber's head.

Open-mouthed, Paul Webb stood transfixed, staring at the ghastly spectacle. Jonah turned his head away. There was no way he could watch. He pushed his way through the crowd that had huddled closer around them, whooping and cheering.

Behind him, a shot rang out. He shuddered as a roar went around the square, then snatched a bottle of whiskey from somebody and took a hard, bitter slug from it.

Amid the whooping, no one paid him any attention. He staggered away from the square around the back of the cabins. Out of sight, he bent over, hands on his knees, tears flooding his eyes.

"Sorry, Ray," he whispered. "There was nothing I could do."

A cold anger surged through his veins. He couldn't stay here any longer. He had to leave right away. He stood up, wiped his eyes, and headed in the direction of the car park.

Reaching the lot, he strode across it to where his silver Nissan was parked on the far side. From the edge of the forest, someone called out to him in a harsh whisper, "*Jonah!* Over here!"

He jerked his head in surprise, and in the moonlight could just make out a figure waving frantically to him. Glancing around to make sure no one was watching, he hurried over.

As soon as Jonah reached him, the man grabbed him by the arm and pulled him behind the tree line. Wordlessly, he led him deeper into the woods, and after twenty yards, the two pulled up behind a large tree.

Jonah stared at the man in astonishment. "Bert! What in the name of *jaysus* are you doing here?"

"I got left behind with Ray Faber," a haggard-looking Bert Olvan told him. "When we were chased into the forest we got separated and—"

"Bert!" Jonah broke in. "They found Ray and dragged him back to the square. Mason killed him."

Olvan nodded grimly. "I know. Bastard thought it was the funniest thing in the world."

Jonah's eyes widened. "You were watching? Where were yeh?"

"I was on the rooftop of one of the cabins overlooking the square." Olvan raised a pair of NV binoculars that dangled on its lanyard by his chest. "I saw everything."

"Why did yeh go and do that?" Jonah asked, confused. "Why not just get the hell away from here?"

Olvan looked at him. "I was watching *you*, that's why?"

Jonah did a double-take. "Me? You knew I was here all this time?"

Olvan nodded. "How do you think I just found you? When I was hiding in the forest earlier, I spotted you on your way back from North Beach. Mason's men were everywhere. I couldn't risk calling out to you, so I ran through the woods to get over to you. By the time I got there, you were walking back to the square with three of Mason's men." He looked at Jonah fiercely. "What the hell are you playing at? Don't tell me you've gone and joined Mason's gang?"

"Of course not!" Jonah retorted indignantly. Then he thought a moment. "Well yeah…kind of, but it's not what yeh think."

"You sure? You looked pretty friendly with everyone back at the square."

"'Course I'm sure. I'm here with you, aren't I? Look, Bert, I need to know if Colleen is okay. You got any news about her?"

Olvan shook his head. "I turned my radio off so I wouldn't risk being heard. By the time I switched it on again, the camp had been evacuated. I'm pretty sure she got off on one of the boats, though."

At the square, there had been no reports of any women killed during the attack. Still, Jonah wouldn't stop worrying until he was certain his wife was safe.

"You still haven't explained yourself properly," Olvan said, looking at him sternly. "What the hell are you doing here with Mason?"

Jonah shook his head forlornly. "When I got back from North Beach, the fighting was over. Like a total gobshite, I thought we'd won and had sent Mason packing. So, happy as Larry, I sauntered over to the square. Lucky for me this geezer Gatto mistook me for one of Nate's crew."

Olvan frowned. "Nate's crew? Who's Nate?"

"He was the leader of the bunch of skangers Mason got to storm North Beach."

"I see. Go on."

Jonah pointed back toward the parking lot. "Gatto took me to the woods on the far side of the car park where he'd killed Nate and three poor other bastards. He was planning to off me too, only he decided to press-gang me into his crew instead."

Olvan's frown grew deeper. "You saying Gatto killed Nate? Why would he do a thing like that?"

"It was an inter-gang thing," Jonah explained. "Happened all the time back in Dublin. Mason promised Wasson Lodge to two different groups, so Gatto took out the competition." He reflected a moment. "I got lucky there. Seeing as I'd just killed the last three geezers who'd know I wasn't part of Nate's group, Gatto wasn't any the wiser."

Olvan's face was becoming increasingly perplexed as he tried to keep up with Jonah's tangential line of reasoning. "Wait...you killed three of Mason's men?"

"Nate's men," Jonah corrected him. "Look, Bert, it's complicated. I'm confused about it meself. Bottom line, Mason thinks I'm part of Gatto's crew, and Gatto is Mason's new best buddy. That's how come I walk around like I please." He pulled out the keys to the Frontier from his pocket. "I've the keys to me Nissan. If you want to risk driving past Mason's checkpoint, I'm game ball for that. Else we hoof it through the forest. What do yeh think?"

"Wait a moment," Olvan said, looking pensive. "Let me figure this out."

"Bert, come on!" Jonah said impatiently. "I need to get back to Colleen."

Olvan shook his head. "I've got a better idea. Something that's going to help us take back this camp." He looked at Jonah. "Something only you can do."

Jonah stared at him in alarm. "Fer feck's sake, Bertie, why does something tell me I'm not going to like this?"

CHAPTER 17

In the smallest of the four upstairs bedrooms, Colleen lay in bed alongside Monica Jeffreys. She could hear her friend's rhythmic breathing as she slept. For Colleen, sleep was an impossibility. Her mind was too plagued by anxiety to allow for such a comfort as that.

Ever since Sheriff Rollins had dragged her onto the very last boat to evacuate the camp, her mind had been in turmoil. Her husband was somewhere back at Camp Benton, and she had no idea whether he was dead or alive. Without a radio, he hadn't been able to contact anyone. She just prayed that he had managed to evade Mason's men when they swarmed the camp, and had gotten away somehow.

Shortly after arriving at the farmhouse, she and Monica had been assigned their room, while in the three larger bedrooms were the rest of the Benton women, along with the group's five children. In a state of shock, Colleen had sat down on the bed, whereupon she'd burst into tears. Until then, she'd managed to keep her emotions frozen, but once in the privacy of the bedroom, it all came flooding out.

Monica had done her best to console her, though there was little she could say or do. The agony of not knowing whether Jonah was alive or not was overwhelming. While part of her accepted there was a distinct possibility he'd been killed, Colleen simply refused to accept it. It was impossible to believe such a vibrant spirit as his was no longer alive.

Besides, she reasoned, her husband was streetwise, alert to every danger. Though trapped on the north headland, surely he would have found a way out, perhaps escaping on one of the boats Mason's men had arrived on. That thought gave her some solace. Tomorrow, she would talk to Walter about organizing a search party to find him.

Exhausted, she finally fell into a fitful sleep as the last of her cogent thoughts flickered across her forebrain.

Jonah Murphy, you better be alive or I'm going to murder you!

CHAPTER 18

The following morning, Rollins awoke to find himself in unfamiliar surroundings. It took him a moment to realize where he was: on a mattress on the floor of a musty smelling room that he shared with four other Benton men.

The previous night, they had been assigned the small annex adjacent to the farmhouse's main living room as their temporary quarters. Walter had promised him that tents would be issued to them the next day so they didn't need to live in such a cramped space.

Two men were still asleep, but Granger's bedroll was empty. He checked his watch. It was 7:15 a.m. Unzipping his sleeping bag, he quickly got dressed and poked his head into the living room, where a few of the others were already up.

"You seen Ned?" he asked them.

"He's in the kitchen, Sheriff," said Jim Wharton, who leaned against the wall sipping a mug of coffee.

Rollins stepped out into the hall and walked down to the kitchen. Inside, two women were preparing breakfast on a camping stove and there was the smell of eggs frying.

Granger sat alone at the kitchen table, a mug of steaming black coffee in front of him. He looked terrible. Unshaved, his hair was disheveled, his pallor an unhealthy gray. Rollins knew just how badly Granger had taken the loss of the camp.

"Been up long?" he asked.

"A couple of hours," Granger replied. "Got sick of staring at the ceiling all night." He indicated to where a small pot sat on top of the counter. "Water's just boiled if you want to fix yourself a coffee."

Rollins unhooked a mug dangling underneath one of the kitchen shelves. He dolloped a heaped spoon of instant coffee into it from a jar nearby, added sugar, then poured the water from the pot.

He sat down at the table and stared at his friend. "Ned, stop beating yourself up over this, you hear?"

Granger's face took on an even more strained expression. "I can't, John. I've spent all night thinking about how I should have handled things differently. Maybe if I'd been quicker to—"

"Ned, stop! Stay focused on how we're going to take the camp back."

Granger managed a weak smile. "Don't worry, I've done plenty of thinking about that too." He checked his watch. "I've arranged a meeting with Walter at nine. I thought it'd be a good idea if our two camps knocked a few ideas around together."

"Excellent idea. Between us all, we ought to come up with something." Rollins paused a moment to reflect. "You know, despite everything, we're not in bad shape. Imagine if Walter and his people hadn't picked us up. We would have spent the night in the forest. No water, no food, low on ammunition. Now *that* would have been bad."

Granger nodded. "True. And that's the scenario Mason probably thinks we're in right now. I don't think he has any idea where we are. We can use that to our advantage."

The front door banged open, then footsteps rushed down the hallway. A moment later, Kit Halpern burst into the kitchen.

"Ned, Sheriff, I've good news!" Halpern shouted excitedly. "Bert's just arrived!"

Rollins looked at Granger, and the two broke out into relieved smiles.

"Where is he?" Granger asked.

"He's outside. He spent the whole night walking here."

Rollins and Granger stood quickly from their chairs and followed Halpern out of the building. The young man took them out to the front garden and over to the next field. Sitting at an empty camping table was Bert Olvan. He rose to his feet as Rollins and Granger approached, who both took turns embracing their friend heartily.

"It's a relief to see you, Bert," Granger said when Olvan finally let go of his bearlike grip. "How on Earth did you know we were here?"

Olvan grinned. "I didn't. I just had nowhere else to go. I prayed you might all make it back here. Tell me, how is the mood?"

Granger shrugged. "Losing the camp has been a big shock to everyone. John's doing a great job keeping everyone's spirits up."

"I'm sure," Olvan replied. "I've some good news. Our Irish friend Jonah Murphy is alive too."

"That's good news indeed!" Rollins looked around. "Where is he? Gone off to see Colleen, I'll bet."

Olvan shook his head. "I persuaded him to stay put. Last I saw of him, he was heading back to the square."

The two men stared at Olvan, confused looks on their faces. "The square...at Camp Benton?" Rollins finally said. "Bert, what on Earth are you talking about?"

A tired smile came to Olvan's lips. "It's a long story. To cut it short, we now have a spy in Mason's camp. Let's make sure we put him to good use."

***

Colleen woke up with a start, and the dull, aching pain she'd felt in her heart all night turned full volume again as she came to her senses. Frail and exhausted, she got out of bed where Monica still lay, fast asleep.

She slowly got dressed and was tying the laces of her boots when there was a light rap on the door. Mary Sadowski poked her head in. "Colleen, you better come outside," she said quietly. "I've some news for you."

Colleen's heart beat fast. She tried to read the expression on Mary's face. It wasn't comforting. "Is it bad? You better tell me."

Sadowski hesitated. "Not exactly. But it's not good news either."

Colleen's lower lip quivered. "Mary, what are you saying? Please, just tell me."

Mary stepped into the room and grabbed her arm. "Come downstairs. It's better if Bert explains it to you."

CHAPTER 19

Jonah woke up in a wretched state. His mouth felt like a piece of old carpet and his head pounded so hard it felt like a crew of Irish navvies were trying to jackhammer their way out of both sides of his skull. He woozily opened his eyes, whereupon harsh sunlight penetrated his brain like shards of glass. Hastily, he closed them again.

He flopped a hand onto his forehead. Shading his eyes, he opened them again, and saw that he lay sprawled on the grass outside one of the cabins on the square. The morning sun beamed down over the rooftops, while all around him the ground was littered with empty beer cans and whiskey bottles.

Several other men lay close by, mouths open and snoring loudly. Looking closer, Jonah recognized the shoulder-length gray hair of one of them. Don Gatto, his new drinking buddy and a stone-cold killer. A shudder ran down his spine. He'd spent the night partying with quite literally the sickest bunch of skangers on the planet.

What were yeh thinking? he groaned to himself. Then the more pertinent question arose. *And what the hell am I still doing here?*

He crawled through the wreckage of his mind, desperate to remember the events of the night before.

Something at the back of his head nagged at him, something that filled him with unease. What, though? He'd drunk so much whiskey that everything was a blur.

Then it all came flooding back. Mason's brutal execution of Ray Faber. How he'd fled the square in disgust, looking to leave the camp. Something had prevented him from going. What in the name of *jaysus* was it?

Jonah bolted upright. He tapped the front pocket of his shorts to confirm that the two-way radio Bert Olvan had given him was still there. Now he remembered everything.

That's what I'm doing here, he groaned inwardly. *I'm a bleedin' spy!*

During their furtive talk in the woods, Olvan had convinced him to stay on at the camp. Seeing as he'd been accepted as one of Mason's crew, it meant he would be in the perfect position to provide vital intelligence to the Bentons. After much argument, Jonah had reluctantly agreed. Anything he could do to help the Bentons would help keep Colleen safe, the thing that mattered most to him in the world.

He checked his watch and saw it was 8:15 a.m. He stumbled to his feet, grabbed his rifle resting against the cabin wall, and tottered out onto the square.

Around the camp, Mason's crew was slowly rising. Jonah passed two men entering the square from the direction of the parking lot, rifles slung over their shoulders. One of them grinned at him as he shambled by. They looked sleepy, but didn't have that bloodshot, hangover look etched on their faces. The men were returning from guard duty, he guessed.

He passed the dining hall. Through the window, he saw that three women had set up a gas stove and were serving breakfast. He caught a whiff of eggs and bacon, and smelled coffee too.

Coffee!

More than anything, that and a glass of cool water was what he needed most in the world.

He pushed through the door and hoarsely asked one of the women for a glass of water. A small, birdlike girl in her twenties with bleach-blonde hair wearing cutoff shorts and flip-flops chuckled as she poured him a large tumbler full of water from a plastic container.

"You had a hell of a night, didn't you?" she said. She poured him out a coffee. "You feeling well enough for ham and eggs?"

"Please, miss," Jonah croaked, then gratefully knocked back the tumbler in three gulps. That was better. His throat loosened up and his tongue no longer stuck to the roof of his mouth, though the *bhoys* with the kango hammers were still working away like good-o inside his skull. He heaped several spoonfuls of sugar into his mug, mumbled his thanks, and sat down at one of the bench tables nearby.

He took a sip from his coffee and placed it down on the table in front of him. Then he pressed the palms of his hands together, closed his eyes, and said a little prayer quietly to himself.

Dear Lord...Brendan Murphy here—you know—Jonah. Look, I know it's been a while, and by rights I shouldn't be asking yeh anything right now, especially not after the amount of gargle I drank last night. But it was me nerves. I hope yeh understand that, and God knows, I'm paying for it now. Ah silly me, you're God, of course yeh know.

Eh...where was I? Ah yeah...please Lord, look over Colleen and make sure she stays safe. That's the thing that matters most to me in the world. After that, if you could spare this auld sinner a few minutes of yer time, I'd be grateful. I'm not such a bad bloke, and I'm hoping yeh might see yerself to help me out of this mess. I don't know how many Hail Mary's it'll take, but I'll rattle one off now. Show yeh I mean business."

Glancing to either side of him, Jonah crossed himself. *"Hail Mary, full of grace...hallowed be thy name..."*

CHAPTER 20

The Benton council met at 9 a.m., convening in the patio area under the shade of the trellis. During the day it was the best place for them to sit, rather than in the stuffy heat of the farmhouse. It offered a little more privacy too.

Almost as soon as they'd sat down, the four members of the Eastwood War Committee appeared, appointed by Walter that morning. Seeing as the discussion at hand was on how to retake Camp Benton, he'd deemed that there was no point in involving anyone else in the talks other than those experienced with weapons.

"Most of you already know Cody," Walter said, introducing his men. "This here is Ralph and Clete. Two key members of our group."

Like most people meeting Ralph for the first time, the expressions of those around the table took on a mixture of surprise and alarm as they observed the tangle of scars that took up almost the entire real estate on his face. The ruby-eyed silver skull that adorned his right hand, along with the Motörhead T-shirt, skinny black pants, and motorcycle boots only added to the effect.

"Good to meet you both," Rollins finally said, before going on to introduce his own team.

"All right, Sheriff," Walter said as he grabbed one of the extra chairs that had been brought out by Rollins earlier and sat down at the table. "How about you guys bring us up to speed on your thoughts about taking back the camp. I'm sure you've already done plenty of thinking about it."

Rollins gestured to Granger, sitting across the table from him. "Ned, take out the map and let's go through the camp layout with Walter and his men. They don't know it as well as we do."

Granger leaned over one side of his chair and produced a brown leather satchel. He opened it up and pulled out a large sketchbook, the type an artist might use. Flicking through the pages, he selected one, then placed the pad at the center of the table.

In thick black marker was a neatly drawn plan of Camp Benton and its surroundings. The group spent the next fifteen minutes going through it in detail, discussing perimeter posts, Papa One through Five, with each of their strengths and weaknesses, the layout of the Ring around the square, both the North and South Beach defensive positions, and the fallback route along which the camp's evacuation had taken place.

"Right now, Mason is probably making some changes. He knows *we* know exactly how everything is laid out," Granger finished up. "That's what I would do in his position. He might well guard the perimeter more securely. Breaking through it was what ultimately led to the camp's fall..." He trailed off as he wrestled with his emotions.

Walter looked up from the map at Granger with a resolute expression. "Listen, Ned, at the moment of our choosing, we'll retake the camp. And when we do, we'll show Mason and his men no mercy, that I can assure you." He glanced over at Mary Sadowski, who gave him a grim nod of approval.

"I appreciate your words, Walter," Granger said, who by now had composed himself. "Speaking of the moment of our choosing, there's been a recent development that might influence any plans we make. Believe it or not, we have a spy in Mason's camp. Someone who will keep us up-to-date with his activities."

Walter stared at him blankly. "A spy in the camp? You've lost me, Ned."

Granger smiled briefly. "Over to you, Bert."

Olvan spent the next few minutes going through the events of the previous night, explaining to Walter and his team how one of their men, an Irishman by the name of Jonah Murphy, had been mistaken for one of Mason's new recruits and was now firmly embedded at the camp.

"How are you communicating with him?" Cody asked once Olvan finished speaking.

"I gave Jonah my radio," Olvan told him. "I'm due to contact him today at noon. Then me and a fellow by the name of Kit Halpern will take turns staying in contact with him."

"These radios only have a short range," Walter told him. "You'll need to find someplace safe where the two of you can change shifts easily."

Olvan nodded. "I know of a good spot near Devil's Point on an abandoned forestry track. We'll be real careful coming in and out on the changeover to make sure no one spots us."

"Good..." Walter said slowly, thinking through the implications of this unexpected news. "You know, with this guy Jonah at the camp, we should also get advanced warning if and when Mason decides to come looking for you guys. Us too, for that matter."

"Absolutely," Granger agreed. "We should work on a few different scenarios around that. Perhaps plan our attack while he's out searching for us. Take it while it's less guarded."

"Great idea. This is guerrilla warfare. We need to start thinking more tactically." Walter tapped the side of his head. "We need to get into Mason's head, start playing against his weaknesses, not his strengths. In this case, his natural aggressiveness."

Ralph, who had been sitting quietly all this time, chose that moment to speak. "I've got another scenario to put on your list, call it the *snake's head* scenario."

Everyone turned and stared at him.

"All right," Rollins said. "How does that go exactly?"

Ralph leaned his bone-hard frame back in his chair and stretched out his long, gangly legs. "From what I've heard about this Mason character, I think I know the type. Hell, even had them as cellmates. A tough guy that rules by fear, but one that's got personality too. It's how come he's managed to build up his gang so quickly. 'Course, in my experience, it's a lot easier to recruit badasses than the good guys."

Sitting beside him, Clete sniggered. "Too much jail time's made you cynical, Ralph, that's all."

The bank robber shrugged. "Can't deny that. One thing I know is that with a guy like Mason, everything centers around him. No one does jack shit without his say so. Whack Mason, and the rest of his gang run around like headless chickens. Makes getting your camp back a whole lot easier." Ralph stared at Rollins. "With your boy Jonah on the inside, we should know the next time Mason intends sticking his nose outside the camp. Put a hit team in place, and *bang!* We ace the mother," he said, clapping his hands loudly. He turned to Mary Sadowski and grinned. "Pardon my language, Miss. Didn't mean to offend."

"None taken," Sadowski replied coolly. "Not in this particular case."

There was an animated look on Granger's face now. "Ralph is correct. From what I saw, Mason's got no real chain of command. If we get advanced warning when he next leaves camp, we can set up an ambush. Give the bastard a taste of his own medicine."

Walter nodded. "'Cutting off the snake's head' is a legitimate war strategy. The trick will be in setting up the roadside ambush just right. We'll need several men in position to spray him with everything they got." A look of concern came over his face. "One thing, though. Something like this is a dangerous undertaking for your guy. What's this Jonah character like? Has he got the mettle for this?"

"I think so," Olvan replied. "As to his character, let's just say he's not the type you meet every day of the week. And he sure talks a lot, don't he, Mary?"

Walter was surprised to see the normally stern-faced Mary crack a dry smile. "You can say that again. Still, he's tough to the core. If anyone can handle himself at Mason's camp, it's Jonah."

CHAPTER 21

Jonah was on his third coffee when Gatto and two of his crew entered the dining hall. The three ordered breakfast at the serving counter, then joined him at the table.

"I was wondering where you got to," Gatto said. He sat down beside Jonah, plonking his coffee mug down in front of him. "Thought maybe you'd run out on me."

Jonah shook his head. "I'm not the ungrateful type. You saved me life last night, remember?"

Gatto smiled. A woozy, half-drunk smile. "Seeing as you put it that way, guess I did." He took a sip from his coffee and winced. "Jesus, did we party last night. My head feels like it got run over by a two-ton truck. Tell me, Murph, how do I look?"

"Like yer fit for the knacker's yard," Jonah told him. "I'd drag yeh there meself, only I don't have the strength."

Gatto chuckled. "I'm not surprised. You look like death warmed up too."

"And that's after three coffees. Yeh should have seen me thirty minutes ago."

After some more banter, three plates of eggs and ham were served up to the new arrivals and they tucked into their food.

"So what's the plan today?" one of the men, a short, wiry man with curly hair and a deeply-lined face, asked. Jonah had spoken with him the previous night, but couldn't recall his name.

"We head back to our camp and pack up our gear. We need to move to the lodge ASAP," Gatto replied, slouching over table and slurping runny fried eggs into his mouth. He lifted his head and looked across at Jonah. "Murph, your camp is over on the north side of the lake, if I remember right."

"Eh, yeah…." Jonah racked his brains. The previous night Gatto had mentioned something about where Mason had found Nate's gang. "Later on, I'll head over to Greasy Spoon Creek and fetch me gear too."

Gatto chuckled. "'Greasy Spoon Creek'. You crack me up. All right, after breakfast we'll go our separate ways and meet back at the lodge. I can't wait to move in. It's got six bedrooms, and Mason told me he left three travel trailers for us there too." He looked around the table, grinning. "We'll be living it up in style, boys."

"How about Mason?" Jonah asked casually. "He got plans for us later?"

"No idea." Gatto nodded in the direction of the serving counter. "But there he is over there. Why don't we ask him?"

Jonah jerked his head to one side to see Mason talking to the skinny birdlike woman. She stood close to him, smiling. It was obvious there was something going on between them.

"Hey, Mason!" Gatto bellowed out. He waved a hand impatiently. "Over here!"

Gatto was obviously one of those brash insensitive types. Jonah wouldn't have dreamed of addressing Mason like that in a million years.

The bandit muttered something to his girl, then came over to the table. "Yeah, Gatto. What do you want?"

Gatto pointed at Jonah. "Murph here wants to know if you have any plans for us today."

Mason looked at Jonah coldly. "What's it to you?" he asked in a surly tone.

"Eh, just wanted to know if we'd be taking it easy today," Jonah mumbled feebly, thinking of the first thing that came to his mind. "After all that gargle last night, I'm totally bolixed. Absolutely in bleedin' bits."

Mason's face turned from a dark frown, to confused, then broke out into a large smile. "You're from Ireland, aren't you? I'd recognize that accent anywhere." Before Jonah could reply, Mason waved his hand toward the counter. "Tania, bring my coffee over here!" he yelled over to the skinny girl. "I'll take it with Murph."

Jonah's heart leaped as Mason grabbed a chair from the next table and sat down opposite him. The last thing he needed was the bandit's direct attention on him. It was hardly keeping the low profile Olvan had instructed him to take.

"To answer your question, today's kickback day," Mason told him. "Tomorrow we go look for the Bentons. If they're foolish enough to have stayed in the area, we'll finish them off."

Gatto nodded approvingly. "Glad you're not the kind of guy who leaves unresolved issues behind. Neither am I."

Mason ignored the comment. Instead, he stared at Jonah keenly. "You know, Murph, my great grandfather was from Ireland. John Joseph Bonner was his name."

"Yeh don't say," Jonah murmured politely, wisely declining to ask the obvious question, whether Jonjo Bonner was a complete skanger like Mason? Odds said he was.

"He hailed from Spanish Point, County Clare. Ever heard of it?"

"I know it well. Beautiful spot "

Mason's eyes lit up. "You've been there? No fucking way!"

Jonah nodded, trying to figure out whether this new development was a good thing or not. "There's good fishing to be had there. Caught meself an eight-pound bass last time I was down. A couple of flounder too."

A delighted Mason slapped the table with the flat of his palm, spilling the coffee Tania had just brought over. "I'll be damned. Ninety-eight percent of the country has fucking croaked it, yet here I am talking to someone from halfway across the world who's been to the very town my ancestors came from."

Jonah smiled. "Looks like it's still a small old world." He paused a moment. "Yeh know why it's called Spanish Point, don't you?"

Mason shook his head. "Never really thought about it...why?"

Jonah was surprised that Mason lacked the imagination to have ever questioned the origins of such an exotically-named place. Despite his initial hesitance, it occurred to him that this was an opportunity to get onto Mason's good side. Who knew where it might lead?

"It's because of the Spanish Armada," he explained. "See, in 1588, one hundred and thirty galleons with thirty thousand men on board set sail to invade England. It was the largest naval invasion fleet ever for its time. Only sixty-seven ships returned. The Spanish got their arses handed back to them on a plate."

Though not the most academic of blokes, Jonah loved history, particularly Irish history. Perhaps that was because he came from a long line of Fenians, and could recite the names of the 1916 martyrs backward since the age of seven. The rest of his school grades had been dire, however, which was why he'd joined the merchant navy at nineteen.

"Oh yeah?" Mason leaned forward in his chair. While he mightn't have been interested in the history of his ancestral home until then, he appeared interested in it now. "So why did the Spanish want to invade England? And what the fuck does that have to do with Ireland?"

"That'll take some explaining. You got the time?"

Mason shrugged. "I like a good war story. Why not?"

"All right, I'll give it me best shot." Jonah settled into his storytelling role, something he was a past master at, even with a raging hangover. "At the end of the sixteenth century, Spain was the most powerful empire on the planet. They ruled half of Europe and all of the New World, where their conquistadors were plundering gold from the Mayans, Aztecs, and Incas, and bringing it all back to Spain. Only problem was that the English—geezers like Francis Drake—kept attacking their ships on their way home to Europe and stealing their loot." He looked around the table. "Yis have all heard of Sir Francis Drake, haven't yis?"

Gatto's wiry companion piped up. "I think so. Didn't Errol Flynn play him once in a movie?"

Jonah grinned. "Fair play to yeh, Curly, he most certainly did. Now Drake was what they called a privateer, basically, a pirate commissioned by the Crown to rob the Spanish blind. Queen Elizabeth…remember, she had the hots for Errol in the movie? Well, she didn't want to use the Royal Navy to attack the Spanish, so she pretended that none of these attacks had anything to do with her. Ah, she was a sneaky wan all right."

Mason was getting the picture. "So the Spanish were stealing the gold from the Aztecs, then Drake was robbing it from them as they sailed back to Spain. That's why the Spanish went to war with England, right?"

Jonah winked at him. "Got it in one, bud. Yep, King Phillip of Spain got pissed off with a shower of English bastards stealing his hard-won treasure. Yeh can't fault the geezer, can yeh?"

Mason chuckled. "I'd be pissed too."

"Well, King Philo goes and assembles this great big fleet and sets sail for England to give the Brits a good spanking. On the way, they stopped at Calais, northern France, where they waited up for more ships to join them before crossing the English Channel. Only thing was, the crafty Brits knew they were coming. They crossed the channel first and floated fire ships downwind into where the Spanish galleons were anchored. You got to remember, back then boats were made of wood. Nothing scared a captain more than a blazing ship heading straight for them."

"So what happened?" Mason asked, transfixed by Jonah's story. "Did they set fire to the fleet?"

Jonah shook his head. "Nope, but they rattled the Spaniards good. Ye've probably heard the term 'cut and run', haven't yis?"

"Sure," Gatto replied. "It's when you got to beat it from somewhere fast." He grinned. "Just like the Bentons did last night."

Inwardly, Jonah winced. "Exactamundo, Gat. It's a naval expression that goes back to those very times. See, in order to escape the fire ships, the Spaniards had to cut their anchor lines to get away from the danger. And when they scattered, the English picked them off. Bleedin' slaughtered them. So badly, in fact, that what was left of the fleet scarpered back to Spain with their tails between their legs, and that was the end of King Philo's invasion of England." Jonah put on a glum face. "More's the pity, too. If they'd succeeded, maybe it wouldn't have taken us Irish another three hundred years to get the Brits off our backs."

Mason frowned. "It's a good story, but I still don't see what it's got to do with Ireland."

Jonah looked at him approvingly. "Now get this…" He leaned forward at the table and slid Gatto's empty plate close to his. "Say these two plates here are England and Ireland." He stuck a finger between them and traced it around the back of one of them. "In order to escape the English, what remained of the expedition force sailed north around Scotland and entered the Atlantic Ocean. Their plan was to head west into the safety of the open seas." Jonah stretched his finger farther out, then swung it back toward the side of the plate. "But as luck would have it, they sailed into a fierce storm that forced them back along the west coast of Ireland." He paused a moment, hovering his finger next to the plate. "Ordinarily that wouldn't have been a problem.

They would have just waited out the storm, then headed west again. But on this occasion, they couldn't. Any guesses why not?"

He looked around the table at the blank faces. "I'll give yis a clue. It was something to do with what happened back in Calais."

Mason and Gatto stared at each other, frowning. Then Mason thumped his fist down on the table. "Goddammit…the anchors!" he said, laughing hard.

Jonah grinned. "Good man!" He looked over at Gatto. "That's why this man here is the boss. See Gat, without their anchors, the Spanish couldn't secure a position and wait out the storm." He rammed his hand into the side of the plate. "They were washed up onto the rocks along the west coast of Ireland, shipwrecked in places such as what is now called Spanish Point in remembrance of the occasion. The very town your great grandfather hailed from, Mason, before coming to America to make his fortune."

Mason looked at Jonah appreciatively. "Helluva story, Murph." He shook his head wistfully. "I always meant to go to Ireland and check out my ancestry. Just never got around to it."

Jonah nodded. "Back home, they used to do great tours for the Yanks…err…youse lot. Not much chance of that now."

"True enough. Still, it's good to have an Irishman at my camp. Makes me feel lucky."

"Hey, I found him first. Murph's with me," Gatto said, half-frowning. Seeing the ferocious glare Mason turned to him with, even the brash Gatto was taken aback. "'Course, neither of us would be here if it wasn't for you," he hastily conceded.

"Damn straight," Mason growled. "You're staying at the lodge at my invitation. Don't ever forget that." He swilled down the last of his coffee and stood up from the table. "Murph, come see me tonight after you settle in at the lodge. We'll talk more about the old country over a drink. Nobody here can keep up with my drinking. Let's see how you fare." With that, he headed back over to Tania and, after speaking with her briefly, exited the dining hall.

After he left, Gatto turned to Jonah. "Can't say I know Mason well, but that's the first time I've seen him laugh. Looks like he's taken a shine to you, Murph."

Jonah managed a weak smile. "Talk about the luck of the Irish, eh?"

CHAPTER 22

By now, everyone at Camp Eastwood was aware of the calamitous events that had taken place the previous night, and all understood the reason for the Benton group's pale, shell-shocked faces. That included the "Georgians", as the recently-arrived recruits from Gainesville were known, though the term amused Simone somewhat, seeing as she was from North Carolina.

The unexpected influx of people forced a change in the camp's sleeping arrangements. Three of the farmhouse bedrooms had been designated for the Georgians - one for Simone and Marcie, another for Laura and Jenny, and the tiny bedroom at the end of the hall for Billy Bingham. Given the circumstances, none objected to camping outside until the Bentons' situation was resolved. It was summertime, and all were content to sleep in tents, pitched under a stand of apple trees in the field adjacent to the farmhouse.

Fred and Eric's situation was different though, and the two had already moved into a utility room next to the kitchen. With easy wheelchair access down the hall, it suited their needs perfectly.

What alarmed everyone far more than any inconvenience was Mason's brutal attack at Lake Ocoee. It served to underscore the reality of their situation. Even for a large group such as the Bentons, danger and menace still lurked. Nowhere was safe in the world anymore.

***

Despite the disruptions, Marcie and Billy were determined to continue with the work at the farm. Billy in particular was anxious to make sure that everything that had been hauled from Willow Spring was put to good use.

That morning, Marcie arranged a scavenge run to Dalton City, Pete having suggested it as her best bet on finding the supplies she needed. None of the men at the camp were available to accompany them, however, as they were all either on defensive duty or undergoing weapons training. Undaunted, Marcie took it upon herself to arrange a security detail, and after breakfast, a heavily-armed group of five women – Marcie and Simone, along with their three new friends, Maya, Emma, and Greta – headed out of the camp in Fred's shot-up station wagon, trailer attached.

The trip took several hours, but was worth it. Thanks to Pete's directions, they found everything they needed.

On their return, Billy ran out to meet them in the front yard, and rooted through the trailer. He was delighted to find, among other items, a kiddie pool, several sheets of plywood, tarpaper, and a stack of wooden roof shingles. The ducks would soon have a new home, and a proper pool to wade in.

The five women, along with Billy, Jenny, and Laura, got to work. They began by bringing in the tiny herb pots Billy had been carefully tending and placing them along the windowsill behind the kitchen sink. Billy instructed Laura on how often they should be watered, and told her that she was now in charge of them.

They then went out into the backyard and over to the vegetable garden, where Marcie handed Greta and Emma two new weeding forks, courtesy of Walmart. Though Emma knew practically nothing about gardening, Greta had grown vegetables in her backyard in Knoxville and made sure that Emma pulled up weeds, not vegetables.

The herb garden was in good shape, and after a few brief instructions, Marcie left Jenny and Laura there to tidy it up. Then Marcie, Billy, and Simone walked through the garden to the old plastic container the ducks were using as their temporary wading pool. Nearby was a galvanized steel pot that Billy had filled with fresh drinking water that morning.

Only a single duck was in sight. After a frantic search, Billy found the rest of them. They'd escaped out the back gate, which someone had left open, and were happily waddling around in the long grasses of the next field.

They dumped the old plastic container and replaced it with the kiddie pool. Then the three took several trips to fetch water from the river, and filled it up. Billy herded the wayward ducks back through the gate, and soon they were all splashing happily in and out of their new pool.

The next task on the list was to make them a shelter. The previous night, they had been kept in the back of Fred's station wagon. While keeping them safe from predators, it was only a short-term solution.

The design of the duck house was simple, identical to the one Billy's father had made back at Willow Spring Farm.

Billy sawed a long sheet of half-inch plywood in two, after which he tacked tarpaper onto both pieces, then nailed on the five-inch cedar shingles. When both pieces were ready, he leaned them up against each other to form an A-framed shape while Simone and Marcie screwed them together.

They used some two-by-two lengths of wood to hold the structure in place, nailed on the back wall, then a front door, complete with a simple latch. Dropping his tools, Billy ran off to the barn and came back with some hay for bedding.

"They'll be happy here," he said, standing up with satisfaction. "Whoever gets up first can let them out each morning."

Marcie smiled. "Let's go fetch Fred and Eric, and start digging the area for the hoop houses. Brace yourselves, it's going to be backbreaking work. We'd better get the rest of the girls on it too."

CHAPTER 23

Jonah woke up from a long nap. Opening his eyes, it took him a moment to remember where he was. In Chickasaw, the cabin he and Colleen had been living in prior to Mason's invasion of the camp.

Earlier, at the dining hall, he had made his excuses with Don Gatto and ambled over to it. When he got there, he was thankful to see no one had claimed the cabin yet. He'd quickly stuffed Colleen's things into her backpack, then stashed it in the forest around the back of the cabin. The last thing he wanted was any of Mason's people getting hold of her possessions.

He wasn't due to meet Gatto at the lodge until that afternoon, so he'd headed back to the cabin and taken a quick lie down to work off the effects of his hangover. Nothing soothed an alcohol-ravaged brain better than sleep.

His nap turned out to be longer than he'd intended, however. Checking his watch, he saw it was 12:20 p.m.

"*Jaypers!*" he yelped, jumping out of the bed in a panic. The previous night, he'd arranged to make radio contact with Bert Olvan at noon that day. He couldn't afford to miss the call.

He hurriedly put on his boots and left the cabin. Checking no one was around, he went around the back of the cabin to where an overgrown footpath led him into the forest. After fifty yards, he stepped off the trail and ducked around the back of a large birch tree.

He pulled out the tiny radio set Olvan had given him and powered it up, making sure the volume was down low. "Bert...you there?" he whispered, then released the Talk button and pressed the radio up to his ear.

There was a slight fizzle, then, *"Yes, Jonah. I'm here. I was getting worried about you, over."*

Jonah breathed a sigh of relief. "Bertie, great to hear yer voice again. Sorry I'm late. I...eh...ran into a spot of bother, that's all."

"What happened? Over."

"I...eh...got held up with Mason. Geezer wouldn't stop yapping to me." Jonah figured it was a close enough version of the truth. Better than admitting he'd been fast asleep with a stinking hangover. "Listen, tell me this and tell me no more...have yeh seen Colleen yet? Is she all right, over?"

Jonah closed his eyes, awaiting Olvan's response.

"Colleen is fine. She's at Camp Eastwood with the rest of our group, over."

Jonah looked up to the heavens and whispered his thanks. "Eastwood? That's that geezer Walter's camp, isn't it?" Other than hearing that it had been down to Walter that Mason had come to the Cohutta, he didn't know much else about the group.

"Correct. They're good people. Any news at your end, over?"

"You better believe it," Jonah replied urgently. "Tomorrow morning, Mason is heading out to look for the Bentons. If he finds yeh, he plans on finishing yis off, over."

There was a brief pause before Olvan spoke again. *"Jonah, this is exactly the kind of information we need from you. It may help us end this situation quickly. You think you can get us more details on his plans tomorrow, over?"*

"I'll try. Like what?"

"Such as what time he'll leave camp. The color and model of the vehicle he'll be driving. Whether he'll be behind the wheel or not. Things like that. Over."

Jonah frowned. "What do yis need to know all that for?"

"We're planning an ambush to take him out. Without Mason in charge, it'll make taking back the camp a lot easier."

Jonah's eyes widened, surprised by how fast the Bentons were moving. Thinking about it, though, it made sense. In football, a team was always the most vulnerable to conceding a goal directly after scoring one themselves. In some respects, this wasn't any different.

"We're only going to get one shot at this," Olvan continued, *"so we'll need accurate intel. Over."*

Jonah cast his mind back to his conversation with Mason that morning, and how he was going to meet him again that evening. Perhaps his little prayer had been answered after all. "All right, I'll do me best. Tell me, Bertie, can I skedaddle the hell out of here after that? I need to get back to Colleen pronto, over."

"Of course. By the way, you reminded me of one other thing. Colleen has a message for you. Let me see if I remember it correctly… Jonah, stay sharp, watch your gob, and get back to me in one piece. PS…I love you very much." Olvan chuckled. *"I think that was everything…over."*

Jonah felt his emotions rising, and he choked up. "Thanks, Bertie. Tell her I love her very much too."

"Roger that. All right, that's enough for now. You need to conserve your battery. Jonah, we're real serious about this plan. Kit and I are going to take turns manning the radio until midnight. You can call us any time until then. Soon as you have any news, you inform us. And stay safe. Got that?"

"Got it. Trust me, Bertie boy, I'm all over this like a bad rash. I can't bleedin' wait to get out of here. Talk to yeh soon. Over and out."

Jonah switched off his radio, shoved it back in his shorts, then headed back toward his cabin, a jaunt in his step.

Things were looking up. His wife was safe and the Bentons had a plan to kill Mason. The sooner the skanger was offed, the sooner he would be back with Colleen. That moment couldn't arrive soon enough for him.

CHAPTER 24

With the news from Jonah Murphy that Mason would soon come looking for the Bentons, Camp Eastwood went on high alert. Under Walter, Ned, and Mary's supervision, its inhabitants worked feverishly all afternoon to bolster the camp's defenses even further. There was no guarantee their ambush plan would succeed, and everyone knew only too well what he and his men were capable of.

As well as fortifying the camp itself, extra observation posts were set up, including one that overlooked the concrete bridge separating Georgia from Tennessee. Whether Mason would travel as far south as the Alaculsy Valley was debatable, but coming from Lake Ocoee, it was the most likely route by which he would arrive.

Once the work was finished, Walter and Ned began planning the "Snake's Head" operation. Unlike last time, they hoped they would strike first.

Both men agreed that an L-shaped ambush would be the most effective, and they planned on deploying the majority of the hit team along the long edge of the "L" as Mason's vehicles drove into the trap. Ahead, along the short edge, a smaller group would be in position to provide an interlocking field of fire without endangering their own men, as well as ensuring that Mason could neither go forward nor retreat.

Six men were assigned to the team. Cody, Clete, Ralph, and Jim Wharton would take up positions along the long edge of the "L", the main kill zone. Cody and Clete would fire 5.56 mm fifty-grain jacketed hollow points. Aimed at Mason's head and upper body, the rounds would mushroom on impact to devastating effect. Alongside them, Ralph and Jim Wharton would simultaneously fire 62-grain steel core, full metal jacket rounds, capable of piercing the door of Mason's vehicle in case he managed to duck below the window in time.

At the short edge of the "L", the crossfire position, Rollins and a man named Sam Kirby would also fire jacketed hollow points through the front window, targeting Mason's head and chest.

The initial planning over, Walter and Granger needed to find the best location for the ambush site. After scouting the area, they decided that the junction of Cookson and Card Spur would be ideal. Two miles south of Camp Benton, there were no turnoffs beforehand that Mason might take, and being a T-shaped junction, it meant he would be forced to slow down as he approached it. It also offered a spiderweb of nearby forestry roads that would allow the team to escape easily.

"It might not appear too complex, but there's a lot of moving parts to this operation," Granger warned the assembled hit team on their return to Camp Eastwood as they sat around the table outside Walter's trailer. Using the detailed sketches the two had drawn, he and Walter had been going through the plan for the past twenty minutes. "Plenty that can go wrong here, trust me."

Walter agreed. "You'd be surprised how one unplanned glitch can turn a simple operation like this into a total clusterfuck."

"Like what?" Cody asked.

"Poor communications, for a start," Walter replied. "We can't afford any misunderstandings. Speaking of which, I will be your spotter on this mission. I'll be in the forest outside the camp's entranceway and will radio you when Mason exits the camp. You'll need to understand my instructions clearly."

"Such as?" Ralph asked.

"Such as confirming Mason's position in the convoy. Jonah may not have time to give us that information in the morning. No point in people risking their necks taking out the wrong vehicle."

"During the time I had the dubious pleasure of being Mason's guest, he always drove a black GMC Canyon," Granger said. "We'll need to confirm that tomorrow, though. Whether he drives himself or sits in the passenger seat is important, too. It'll affect the configuration of the ambush."

"Why?" Cody asked, looking slightly confused.

"Better to shoot from the side of the road that Mason is sitting on," Clete explained. "Gives us a better chance of killing him."

Walter nodded. "Most likely Mason will be driving, so your starting position will be on the left side of the road. Depending on Walter's signal, though, you may need to cross over. Don't worry. There's good cover on both sides." He looked around at the men. "From start to finish, the attack won't take more than thirty seconds. The trick will be to make sure Mason enters the kill zone without any twitchy fingers giving the game away. Once you've targeted his vehicle and shot him to hell, you're out of there."

Like Granger had said at the outset, though straightforward, the operation had a lot of moving parts. For the next while, the two ex-soldiers continued to drill the team, going through every minute detail of the plan, including the different scenarios depending on where Mason's vehicle would be positioned in the convoy, how tightly bunched his vehicles would be, the exact position each shooter would take during the attack, and the various radio commands they could expect to receive from Walter. Also of huge importance, the rally point and escape route by which they would exit the area.

Finally, Walter and Granger were satisfied with their preparations. They wrapped things up, and the hit team traipsed over to the farmhouse, where the evening's dinner was being prepared.

It would be another early night for them. The following morning, they would rise at 5 a.m. and head down to the ambush site. While it was unlikely Mason would head out of camp that early, they couldn't afford to take the chance and get caught off guard.

"So, what's your thoughts?" Granger asked Walter while the two stood together on the patio beside the grill. "You think we've got a realistic shot at this?"

"Absolutely," Walter replied, as the smell of sizzling venison steaks wafted under their noses. "If your man Jonah can find out a little more information for us tonight, even better. The more we know, the greater the chance of this going smoothly. Plus a little luck," he added. "Every military operation needs a little luck to succeed."

Granger smiled briefly. "Me and you have too many missions under our belts to think different. Nothing ever goes totally to plan. Clusterfucks abound."

CHAPTER 25

Jonah sat at the stern of a sixteen-foot Beavertail chugging across the bay, keeping a steady hand on the skiff's outboard tiller. The late afternoon sun hung low in the sky, and a light breeze ruffled his hair. It was another beautiful midsummer's day.

He sighed wistfully. This was only his second time out on the lake since his arrival, and under normal circumstances would be his idea of heaven. Unfortunately, instead of partaking in a few delightful hours of fishing, he was navigating his way toward the western shores of Lake Ocooe, where a bunch of cutthroat bandits awaited his return.

After finishing up his radio call with Bert Olvan, he'd returned to Chickasaw, where he packed up his gear and headed over to North Beach. After a ten-minute search, he'd found the skiff Nate and his team had arrived in the previous night, the one he'd ostensibly come over on. Though he had no idea where Nate's camp was located, he thought it best to make a pretense of going over to Greasy Creek to collect his belongings.

Curiously, while he'd been searching for the skiff, as he'd rounded the point of one of the headland's many tiny bays, he'd spotted Mason and another man dragging a small boat into the forest. They hadn't seen him, and he made sure to quickly duck out of sight before they did. What was that all about?

He reached the far side of the lake, turned south, and soon passed the jutting headland of Camp Benton, though it was perhaps wiser to call it "Camp Mason" for the moment. A few minutes later, he steered the craft into a perfectly-shaped horseshoe bay, from which the impressive Wasson Lodge could be seen.

On the back lawn, Gatto and three of his crew members lay sprawled on deck chairs. Two were bare-chested, wearing swimming shorts and sunshades. They looked more like city tourists on a weekend break than the ruthless bandits who had only the previous night overrun a well-defended camp. Only the semi-automatic rifles that leaned up against the side of their chairs gave the game away. Farther back, another two crew members were chucking a football back and forth to one another. There was no sign of Paul Webb anywhere.

Gatto lifted his head and waved over to Jonah as he tied up to the jetty. "Hey, Murph! Get your ass over here!" he yelled.

Jonah grabbed his backpack off the skiff's deck, hopped up onto the jetty, and made his way over. Ten yards out, Gatto leaned over to one side of his deckchair. A moment later, a small cylindrical shape came whizzing at Jonah, which he caught deftly in one hand.

Gatto grinned. "Nice catch."

Jonah cracked open the can of Coors one-handed and took a long slug from it. The gang leader looked pleased to see him, perhaps even relieved he'd shown up. After all, Jonah had been pretty much press-ganged into his services the previous evening.

He gestured to the empty deckchair beside him. "Sit," he said. "Lenny won't mind you stealing his chair awhile."

"Don't mind if I do." Jonah shrugged the pack off his shoulder and slung it on the ground, then sat down beside Gatto.

"What took you so long?" Gatto asked, staring at him closely. "You hang out with Mason some more?"

Jonah noted an edge to his voice. It appeared Gatto was a little wary of his burgeoning friendship with Mason. He put it down to natural rivalry between the two gang leaders. Growing up in the inner-city flats of Dublin, he'd seen it a dozen times. It rarely ended well. Hopefully it wouldn't this time either.

He shook his head. "Nah, after I left yis, I went and took a quick kip in one of the cabins."

Gatto frowned. "A kip? What the fuck is that?"

"A nap," Jonah explained. "Did me head wonders. Feel fresh as a daisy now."

Gatto grinned. "Me and the boys have been dozing off all day too." He pointed over at the skiff. "That Nate's boat?"

Jonah nodded. "I took it to Greasy Creek and picked up me gear. Thought I'd bring it back here rather than leave it at Mason's camp," he added quickly.

Gatto looked pleased. "Good. It'll come in useful. We left our boat at our old camp and drove back in our trucks. Tomorrow, we'll take yours to cross the bay and pick it up."

Jonah took another slurp from his beer. "Where's Paul and Curly?" he asked, looking around.

Gatto indicated toward the lodge. "They're on guard duty. The last owners built sandbag positions on either side of the building. I posted one at each."

Jonah nodded. "How about accommodation? I bet ye've all taken the good rooms, haven't yis?"

"First come, first served," Gatto replied with a chuckle. "I took a bedroom suite in the lodge. So did most of the boys." He swiveled his head and pointed over to three trailers that sat parked in the center of the field. "The blue trailer is empty, and there's still a room left at the lodge too. Take your pick."

Jonah thought for a moment. "I'll take the trailer," he said. It would give him more privacy, and also offered him a better means of escape when the time finally came.

Gatto nodded. "It's all yours."

Jonah gulped down the last of his beer, then stood up. "I better claim it before anyone changes their minds. See yeh in a few." He picked up his backpack and sauntered off in the direction of his trailer.

"Hey, Murph!" Gatto called out to him. Jonah stopped and turned around. "Glad you showed up. Thought you might have left me to join Mason's crew."

Jonah beamed a big grin back at him, then shook his head emphatically. "No way, Gat. Youse lads fit me style bang on. I'm not going anywhere."

After moving into his new quarters, Jonah spent the rest of the day by the lakeside, chatting with Gatto, horsing around with his men, and learning American football, which he insisted wasn't a "proper" sport at all—too much bleedin' stopping and starting.

Other than for Paul Webb, Gatto and his crew still made him uneasy. The lawless world in which they now found themselves appeared to have stripped them of their humanity. Or perhaps they had always been like that, it was impossible to know. Either way, Jonah's streetwise upbringing had taught him how important it was to chum up to his new friends, and he used all his charm and humor to ingratiate himself with them.

At sunset, they ate dinner out on the lawn. It consisted of cuts of well-hung venison the gang had brought back from their old camp, which they cooked on a grill along with some bockwurst-style hot dogs from out of a bottle.

"Shame there's no rolls for these hot dogs," Curly grumbled as he speared the last one off the grill. Dunking it in a jar of mustard, he took a large bite. "It's stuff like that I miss about the old days."

Jonah raised the can of beer he held in his hand. "I can live without the bread rolls, Curly. What are we going to do when the gargle runs out? That's the nightmare scenario."

Curly chuckled. "Lucky for us, there's still plenty of it around. It's not exactly high on most people's survival list."

Jonah grinned. "True. Yeh can't live on booze alone. Trust me, I've tried."

"The food's already disappeared from the supermarket shelves," Paul Webb said, standing next to Jonah at one side of the grill. Both he and Curly were off duty now, replaced by Lenny and another of Gatto's men. "Gas stations will run dry soon and we'll have to walk everywhere."

"That reminds me," Gatto said. "We should stock up on more fuel soon. I think we're down to out last few jerry cans. Maybe we can find a tank truck and drive it back here," he mused. "Tomorrow we'll make a run to Cleveland and see if we can find one."

"That'd keep us going awhile," Jonah agreed, though privately he doubted they would have much luck finding one. He checked his watch and made a face. "Ah, bollix! Just remembered…I better go and see Mason. He wants another natter about the auld sod."

Gatto scowled. "Don't he have no one else to talk to? He better not make a habit of this."

Jonah gazed at him apologetically. "It's not like I want to, Gat." He hesitated a moment. "Yeh know what? Fuck him, I'll stay. Tomorrow morning I'll tell him I forgot."

Gatto shook his head. "Nah, we can't afford to piss him off. Not for now." He put his arm affectionately around Jonah's shoulder and stuck his face up close, his breath reeking of beer. "Go tell the fucker a couple of bedtime stories, then get back here as soon as you can. You're one of us now, Murph, you hear?"

"I'm with yeh all the way, Gat. Through thick and thin." Unlatching Gatto's arm, Jonah grinned. "Stay up for me. Maybe I'll tell yeh a bedtime story too when I get back."

He strolled up the pathway around the east side of the lodge. After stopping to chat with Lenny a few moments, he pulled out his Maglite and headed down the driveway, the bright beam from his tiny flashlight leading the way. At the bottom, he turned right onto Cookson Road and walked in the direction of Camp Benton, less than a mile away.

He was jittery about meeting Mason again, and focused his mind on what he needed to find out for Bert Olvan. Though straightforward, he had to be careful on how he phrased his questions. Mason was no fool. If, for whatever reason, the bandit wasn't killed the following day, suspicion might easily fall on him. Judging by Ned Granger's experience, that wouldn't work out too well for Jonah.

Halfway up Camp Benton's driveway, two guards stopped him at what had been the camp's Papa Three post, where the eight-wheeler still blocked the road. One of the men recognized him and, after radioing ahead, allowed him pass through.

When he arrived at the square, there was no sign of Mason. Asking around, he was directed to the east side of the camp, where he crossed a wooden bridge spanning a small stream. He found Mason sitting outside a trailer parked at one corner of a large rectangular field. Three more trailers occupied the other corners, and nearby was a cluster of family-sized cabins where other members of Mason's crew sat out as well.

On the table in front of Mason were a bottle of Jim Beam and a two-liter bottle of Coke. Opposite him sat a large pasty-faced man with thick, jet black hair who Jonah recognized from the night before.

Spotting him, Mason leaned back in his chair and hollered out over his shoulder, "Tania, Murph's here! Bring out another tumbler, and some more nuts while you're at it." He gestured for Jonah to sit at the empty chair at the table.

As soon as he sat down, Mason pointed across to the other man. "This here is Doney, my bodyguard and drinking companion. Only, when it comes to drinking he don't keep up with me too good. Do you, Doney?"

Doney grinned, embarrassed. "I thought I could hold my liquor until I met you."

At that moment, Tania came down the trailer steps with a ten-ounce glass and a side plate heaped with cashew nuts. She smiled briefly at him as she placed the items on the table, then headed back into the trailer again. Jonah wondered what she saw in someone like Mason. Safety? Comfort? A sensitive, loving relationship? He very much doubted that.

Mason indicated to the whiskey bottle. "No need to be shy. Help yourself," he said gruffly.

Jonah leaned forward and unscrewed the cap from the whiskey bottle. He poured himself a generous shot, then put the same amount of Coke in. The plastic bottle was cool to the touch. Tania had obviously kept it in the lake earlier.

He raised his glass. "Cheers, lads," he said, then took a long slug. Behind the sweetness of the Coke, the whiskey stung the back of his throat, and he could sense his body greedily sucking the alcohol into his bloodstream. With a satisfied smack of his lips, he placed the now half-full tumbler back down on the table again.

Mason looked across at Doney, grinning. "Looks like I might have some competition tonight. What do you think?"

Doney shrugged indifferently. "We'll see."

Glass in hand, Jonah looked around at his surroundings. "Yeh got yourself a nice setup here, Mason. I see yeh decided to stay in yer trailer instead of taking one of the cabins here? Looks like yeh got a fancy one too."

"I hauled it up from the lodge this morning," Mason replied. "It's way more comfortable than any of the cabins here. Keeps Tania happy too."

Jonah nodded sagely. "No point in getting on the wrong side of your woman. Nothing good ever comes of that."

"Sounds like the voice of experience. So, what happened to your old lady? vPox take her out?"

133

Jonah hesitated. "She's in Ireland. Last time I talked to her, she was fine. But that was two weeks ago."

"How come you were in the US when the shit went down?" Doney asked curiously. "Business?"

"Nah, I was on me holliers in Orlando. Came over with five other geezers on a fishing trip and was the only one to survive." He shook his head wistfully. "Never got out on the water to catch that marlin either."

Mason chuckled. "You'll have to make do with Lake Ocoee catfish instead." He paused briefly. "Orlando? That's a long way from the Cohutta. What made you come all the way here? There's plenty of wilderness areas in Florida. Hell, you could have even camped in the Everglades.

Jonah shuddered. "The Everglades...yikes!" He pinched his freckled forearm. "Look at me. I'm not built for the heat. Nope, I picked meself up a nice jammer and headed north. It's hot here, but a whole lot better than Florida."

"A jammer?" Doney asked with a confused look.

"A car," Jonah explained. "Comes from Cockney rhyming slang, but us Paddies like to use it too."

Mason stared at him blankly. "Cockney rhyming slang?"

Jonah grinned. "Jam jar...car. Jammer for short. Geddit?"

Mason looked across at Doney, and the two broke out into broad smiles. "Not yet. But the night's still young. We'll figure it out."

"I'll say this for the Yanks," Jonah continued. "Youse lot love to drive around in *huuuge* pickup trucks, don't yis? They must do something awful to the gallon. Back home, I drove a Toyota Corolla. Poxy little thing so it was, but at least it didn't cost much to run."

Doney picked up his glass and took a sip. "Trucks are part of the American way, especially out in the boonies. Me, I got myself a nice Ford F-150." He chuckled. "Traded in my ten-year-old one for it before we left Knoxville."

Mason nodded. "I got a GMC Canyon. Like Doney, I choose American. Always."

Jonah scrunched up his face. "Don't think I know that model. Is that the blue truck out in the lot?"

"Nope, it's black. The one with the red sign on the grill."

"Ah, yeah. I think I know the one you mean."

Bingo. Mason drove a black Canyon. Jonah would wait awhile until gleaning the next piece of information. He didn't want to appear too obvious. In the meantime, he took another slug of whiskey.

Forgive me, Lord, this is work, not play. I need to do this.

"All right, Murph," Mason said. "How about you tell us something more about Ireland. Doney's Italian, but he'll listen anyway. It's not like he's got anything better to do."

Jonah shrugged. "Sure, what do you want to know?"

"When I was a kid, my granddad used to tell me stories about how the Irish rebels fought the English. You got anything like that?"

Jonah rubbed his hands gleefully. "Does the pope know how to say a prayer? I got rebel stories coming out me ears. Of Fenians, of Volunteers, of the Rebellion of 1798, and the Easter Rising of 1916 where our brave forefathers fought the British Crown."

He leaned forward in his chair and ushered Mason and Doney in conspiratorially. "Now lads, did either of yis ever hear of the Battle of Vinegar Hill? No? Well listen up and I'll tell yeh it the way me very own grandfather used to tell it to me. It's a terrible tale where innocent Irish men, women and children were slaughtered in droves, so don't feel ashamed if it makes you teary eyed, I've shed many a tear over it meself."

CHAPTER 26

Outside Mason's trailer, the gang leader and Jonah were in animated conversation. A second bottle of whiskey sat on the table while at the far end, a glassy-eyed Doney no longer made any attempt to keep up with the evening's proceedings. His head drooped, and he looked like he might collapse at any moment.

Jonah, however, had no problems keeping up with Mason, and for the past couple of hours, both the flow of liquor and words had been non-stop. Though ruthless and violent by nature, Mason was a surprisingly good listener and had lapped up Jonah's wild yarns of the old country with gusto.

After recounting the Battle of Vinegar Hill, Jonah had gone on to relate several stories of his own forbear's clashes with the Black and Tans, brutal irregular soldiers sent to Ireland by the British during the War of Independence. After that came a tale of the Murphy clan's involvement in the ensuing civil war. Like many countries, having won independence from their colonial masters, Ireland had gone on to fight a bitter internal war.

Finally, the conversation moved on to the topic Jonah had been patiently waiting for.

Reaching for the bottle of Jim Beam, the bandit poured out another shot for the two men. "Better make this one our last. We've an early start in the morning."

Jonah grinned. "Should be a fun day. Are yeh sure the Bentons are still in the area, though? If they've any sense, they'll have bolted somewhere far away from here by now."

"They're still here," Mason said emphatically. He took a sip from his drink. "I'll say one thing for the sheriff, he's not a quitter. Saw that in his eyes the one time I met him. Neither is Ned Granger, his second-in-command. A tough bastard through and through. Kept him prisoner two days, so I ought to know."

Jonah raised an eyebrow. "He was your prisoner? How come?"

Mason explained how a few days ago he'd ambushed and killed three Benton men and taken Granger hostage, and how Sheriff Rollins had rescued him, taking one of his own men prisoner in return, who he subsequently executed. Jonah had heard the story from Bert Olvan, but made sure not to give anything away.

Mason then went on to recount how he'd originally come to the Cohutta in search of a man named Walter, someone he'd tangled with back in Knoxville. By now, his earlier good humor had dissipated, to be replaced by a dark, brooding air. Mason quite obviously held serious grudges, the type of person who would never rest until he'd eliminated each and every potential threat. At that moment, his focus was on Sheriff Rollins and Walter, at whose camp Colleen was currently sheltering. The thought made Jonah increasingly uneasy.

"The two groups are tight," Mason continued. "My men spotted Walter visiting here yesterday morning. My guess is that the Bentons are with Walter's people right now. After all, where else would they have fled to after here?"

"Makes sense. You got any idea where Walter's camp is?"

Mason shook his head. "Somewhere south of here is all I know." He leaned forward in his chair, his hard black eyes boring into Jonah's. "It might take a few days, but I'm going to find it. When I do, I aim on killing two birds with one stone. Rollins and Walter are dead men walking."

Jonah lifted his tumbler and saluted him. "I'll drink to that."

In reality, Mason's comment had sent a shiver down his spine. If the ambush in the morning failed, Mason would soon find Camp Eastwood, putting Colleen in immediate danger. He couldn't have that. Despite the amount of whiskey he'd consumed, a cold sober question entered his head. Why take the risk of the ambush failing in the morning? Why not kill Mason now and take his chances in getting away?

He glanced casually to either side of him to see that many of Mason's men were still outside their cabins and trailers, likewise drinking and talking. He wouldn't stand a hope in hell of making it past the perimeter. His mind raced. Perhaps he could dart into the forest and lose them somehow. Getting off the headland without being spotted would be difficult, though. His odds weren't great.

A better alternative occurred to him. He would wait and see whether the Benton ambush succeeded in the morning. If not, he would find a more suitable opportunity to dispatch Mason, one that offered him a better chance of getting away. With a little guile, Jonah was confident he could arrange that. In the meantime, he needed to glean more information.

"How many men will you take tomorrow?" he asked casually.

"We'll take three trucks. Six men in each," Mason replied. "Gatto will lead the convoy. I'll go next, followed by a trailing vehicle. That's enough security to go find Walter's camp. After that, we'll make plans to attack it in full force."

Jonah stared at Doney, who moments ago had keeled over. He lay slumped over the table, his head resting across his folded arms. "You sure he'll be in shape to drive tomorrow?" he asked with a grin.

Mason jerked a thumb back at himself. "I'll be driving. Used to do it professionally for a private security firm. It's where I met Doney. That's why I trust him more than anyone else in my crew, even if he can't drink for shit." He kicked Doney's foot under the table. "Hey, you drunk fuck. You're supposed to be protecting me!"

Doney lifted his head off the table, his eyes glazed over and unfocused. "Say what, boss?"

"Aw, nothing. Go back to sleep." With a chuckle, Mason turned to face Jonah again. "You know something, Murph? I like you. I'm officially making you a member of my crew. Tomorrow morning, you ride with me. How's that sound?"

Jonah gulped. *Bleedin' diabolical* was how it sounded. The last place he wanted to be the next day was in Mason's vehicle when it got shot to hell. It appeared he'd been too successful in getting close to the bandit.

He smiled weakly. "Great! I don't think Gatto will be too happy about it though."

"Like I give a damn," Mason growled. "He won't kick up about it. Not if he knows what's good for him. You're with me now and that's that."

He knocked back the last of his whiskey and rose from the table. Leaning over, he slapped Doney roughly across the top of the head. "Wake up! Funtime's over. Go get some sleep. I need you sharp in the morning, you hear?"

Doney stood groggily to his feet. Without a word, zombie-like, he lumbered off in the direction where, presumably, his cabin was located.

Mason gave Jonah a brief nod. "Tell Gatto to meet me at the dining hall at 8 a.m. with five of his men. I'll see you there too. Don't forget to pack up your stuff. Remember, you're with me now."

"Sure, boss. See you in the morning."

140

Mason headed toward the steps of his trailer. As soon as his back was turned, Jonah checked his watch. It was 11:55 p.m. Whoever was manning the radio at Devil's Point would be knocking off in a few minutes. He was anxious to give his update right away. His life depended on it.

Crossing the wooden bridge again, he hurried back to the square, empty of people when he reached it, and passed the Art & Crafts room, its yellow sign painted brightly across the doorway. It was the last cabin on the southwest corner, and the footpath ended there. Taking a quick look to either side of him, he stumbled through thick undergrowth and into the forest.

After twenty yards, he stopped and rested against a tree. Though it was a risky place to make his call, he'd no time to get anywhere safer. Breathing hard, he pulled out his walkie talkie, turned it on and jabbed his finger down on the Talk button. "Bert…Kit," he whispered. "Anybody there?"

"*Receiving you loud and clear, Jonah. This is Kit, over.*"

"Kitser, thank God you're still here. I've something important to tell yeh." Slurring his words and out of breath, Jonah concentrated hard on what he had to say. "Now…what was it?"

"*Are you all right, Jonah? Over.*"

"Kit, I'm drunker than a barrel full of monkeys, but for once in me life I can honestly say I was only doing me duty. Wait a sec while I get me head together."

A chuckle came over the airwaves. "*Take your time. It'll come to you.*"

Jonah focused hard. "Mason will be leaving the camp at eight in the morning, so yis better be ready for him then. Do yeh roger me, over?"

"*8 a.m. Copy that. You find out what vehicle he'll be driving, over?*"

"'Course, it's the first thing I asked. It's a black Ravine. Nah, that's not right. It's a…a…black Crevasse. Ah, shite, I've forgotten the name of the poxy thing!" Jonah banged his head against the tree in frustration. It had been earlier in the evening when Mason told him the make of his pickup truck. For the life of him, he couldn't remember it now.

"*Is it a Canyon?*" Halpern asked calmly. "*That's what he drove last time, over.*"

"That's it, a black Canyon!" a relieved Jonah whispered excitedly. "Listen to me, Kitser. Mason and his crew will drive out in three pickups. Six men per truck. You do the maths, I don't think I could even do me two times table right now."

"*Copy that. He'll be in a convoy of three pickup trucks. Six men in each truck makes eighteen in total. What else you got, over?*"

"Mason will be behind the wheel of the second pickup. Here's the kick in the bollix though, I'm going to be riding along with him, so yis better be real careful with yer shooting, yeh hear me?"

There was a pause on the line. "*Copy that. Mason will be driving the second truck. You'll be in it with him. You got any idea where you'll be sitting? Front or back? Over.*"

Jonah thought for a moment. "Probably in the back. His bodyguard, geezer by the name of Doney will most likely be in the front. I can't swear to it though."

"*Got it. Anything else?*"

"Yeh better believe it. Tomorrow morning, I'll be slinging me arse in the bacon slicer for yis, so yeh better not riddle me full of holes. I want to get back to Colleen in one piece. Yeh copy that, over?

There was another pause on the line before Halpern spoke again. "*Jonah, I think it's best if you make contact with us again at 6 a.m. In case there's any change of plan. We need to do everything we can to keep you protected, over.*"

Halpern's words made Jonah breathe a little better. "Yer a sound man, Kitser, I'll do that. Righty ho, I better leg it. People will be wondering where I am. Jonah Murphy signing off. Over and out."

Job done, Jonah powered off the radio and headed back toward the square. When he reached the edge of the forest, he took a quick peek around to make sure the coast was clear, then hands in pockets, strolled off in the direction of the camp driveway.

He thought hard, more sober now. If Gatto was still up when he got back to the lodge, he would give him Mason's instructions for the morning. Also, how he'd been forced to leave Gatto's crew to join him. It was sure to ratchet up the tension further between the two gang leaders.

Who knew? Perhaps Gatto might kill Mason and save everyone the bother. More likely, though, would be that he'd be sitting in the back of Mason's truck as it drove into a deadly trap, with a stinking hangover to boot. He let out a sigh.

Luck of the Irish, eh?

CHAPTER 27

At 4 a.m., Granger, Walter, and the six members of the Snake's Head hit team convened in the farmhouse kitchen. It was still dark outside, and a kerosene lamp had been placed on the table to illuminate the room. On the gas hob in the corner, a large pot of water was coming to the boil. The sleepy group, who'd been roused from their beds an hour earlier than scheduled, were all in need of a strong coffee.

Mugs in hand, they sat down at the table. Granger looked around at them. "People, we got a problem. Late last night we received information that brings today's mission into question. At the very least, it changes the manner in which we conduct it."

With a brief nod, he passed it over to Kit Halpern. The young man went on to detail his radio communication with Jonah Murphy the previous evening, finishing up by explaining how the Irishman would be riding in the same vehicle as Mason when he left camp in a few hours' time.

Clete was the first to react. "Damn," he said. "We can't go shooting the crap out of Mason's pickup with your boy Jonah inside, now can we?"

"Exactly," Walter replied. "Which is why Kit had the good sense to arrange another radio call with him this morning. If we go ahead with this, we need a new plan.

Something more surgical that doesn't endanger Jonah." He glanced at Granger. "Ned and I were thinking that if we can force Mason's vehicle to come to a stop at the Card Spur junction, we can put a sniper in place to take him out."

"How will you get him to stop?" Ralph asked.

"Mason will be in the second vehicle of a convoy of three. If we take out the first vehicle as it approaches the junction, it should force him to stop. Of course, everything depends on certain variables, like how tightly bunched the vehicles are, how quickly Mason reacts to the situation.... Still, it's a simple plan, and easy to execute. Maybe we get lucky and can line up a kill shot."

Clete frowned. "If you force the first vehicle to stop, it means we got no frontal shot. We can only shoot Mason through the driver side window. It's going to be hard to position a sniper unless you know exactly where he's going to stop. Every additional foot he rolls past or pulls up short, leaves a tighter angle to shoot from."

Jim Wharton leaned forward at the table, frowning too. "That's not the only problem. Most likely Jonah will be sitting in the back, but that's not one hundred percent certain. If he's sitting beside Mason, he'll be right in the firing line."

"I'm a good shot," Cody said. "If Mason comes to a stop in front of me, I'm pretty sure I can kill him with a clean shot."

"Pretty sure isn't good enough," Rollins said emphatically. "It only takes Mason to move his head a couple of inches and you'll hit Jonah. I don't want to have to explain to his wife how we missed the bad guy and killed her husband instead."

Wharton shook his head. "Me neither. No way."

There was silence around the table a few seconds while the group reflected on the situation. Then Ralph said, "How about we use the drug cartel's favorite method of assassination? Put two *sicarios* on a motorbike. Driver roars up to Mason's window, guy at the back aces him, and they hightail it out of there." He paused a moment as he thought about it some more. "The trick will be to neutralize Mason's shooters first, otherwise it'll be too dangerous for the riders."

Granger liked the idea. "A motorbike hit gives us more flexibility than a fixed sniper position. From a couple of feet, the shooter's not going to miss either. Let's see if we can figure a way to make this work."

For the next twenty minutes, the hit team worked through various strategies, searching for one that would allow a motorcycle to ride up close to Mason's side window with minimum risk to the riders. Finally, they came up with something they were convinced might work. It was complicated, though, and required the precise execution of certain prerequisite steps. If any one step failed, they would have to abort the operation.

"With a bit of luck, this might just work," Walter said, staring down at several detailed sketches of the ambush site. He straightened up and looked around the room. "All we're missing now are two people crazy enough to volunteer as *sicarios*."

Ralph shrugged. "Seeing as I'm not too particular on someone else riding my Harley, I'll volunteer as the driver."

"I'll do the hit," Cody said. "It's only fair. I'm part of the reason why Mason is in the Cohutta in the first place."

Walter looked at him with concern. "You sure, Cody? I know you're cool under pressure, but we're talking real dangerous shit here."

"Totally," Cody answered firmly. "Besides, *somebody's* got to do this. We might not get another chance before Mason finds our camp."

"Kid, you plug Mason good," Ralph said. "I'll make sure we get away. We'll blast past them with the wind in our hair before they even know what's hit them. Deal?"

Cody grinned back at him. "Deal."

CHAPTER 28

At 8 a.m., Jonah, along with Don Gatto and five other members of his crew, trudged into Camp Benton's dining hall. Jonah felt awful. His mouth was dry as an oatcake, his hands were clammy, and the back of his t-shirt was soaked in sweat—the result of yet another night's heavy drinking.

The anxiety of what was soon to transpire didn't help either. At 6 a.m., he'd had a brief conversation with Bert Olvan, who'd instructed him to sit in the back seat directly behind Mason, if he could, when the convoy left camp. Hungover and sleepy, he hadn't questioned him. Thinking about it now though, it puzzled him. Surely the Bentons would line themselves along the left side of the road, allowing for a clear shot at the driver position. That would make the right-hand side of the vehicle the safer place to sit, not behind Mason. He just hoped they knew what they were doing.

He glanced over at Gatto, wondering what he might say when Mason showed up. On Jonah's return to Wasson Lodge the previous evening, the gang leader and three of his men were still up. They were down at the lakeside playing dominoes on a small foldout table that had been dragged out from somewhere.

He'd sat down beside them at an empty stool. "Well lads, tomorrow's hunt for the Bentons is still on," he said after a few pleasantries. "We need to meet Mason in the dining hall at 8 a.m. sharp. Armed and dangerous."

"Not a problem," Gatto grunted, staring down at his three remaining tiles. He tipped one over and slid it across the table, joining it to one end of the chain.

"Dammit, Gat. You've gone and blocked me," Lenny moaned, sitting to his left. He rapped the table with his knuckles, signaling for play to pass to the next man.

Gatto chuckled. "That's the name of the game, Len." He looked over at Paul Webb sitting opposite him. "How about you, Pauly? You got a move?"

"Sure do." Webb slid out a tile, leaving him with only one remaining. "Watch out. Next turn, I'm chipping out."

"Gat..." Jonah said haltingly, "Mason told me I have to move to his camp in the morning. I'm to join his crew."

Gatto turned sharply in his seat. "What the fuck! You better not have agreed to that. Not without my permission," he said furiously.

Jonah's expression grew more apologetic. "It was an order. What was I to do?" He stared at Gatto glumly. "I like it here with you guys. You think you can have a word with him in the morning?"

"Damn straight I will," Gatto said between gritted teeth. He flung his two remaining tiles across the table, scattering the rest of the pieces in all directions. "Fucker's got no right stealing my men like that."

Jonah left it at that. From the look on Gatto's face, there was no need to say anything more. The mood at the table soured, and a short time later, the group broke up for the night.

As he headed back to his cabin, Jonah chuckled to himself. Both Gatto and Mason had explosive personalities, a recipe for confrontation if ever he'd seen it. Things might get interesting in the morning.

***

At 8:15 a.m., Mason strolled into the dining hall, accompanied by a sleepy-eyed Doney and two members of his crew. Spotting Gatto and his men, he came over to their table. "All set?" he asked.

Gatto nodded sullenly, barely looking up at him. "Yeah, we're ready."

"Good." Mason checked his watch. "See you at the parking lot in ten minutes. I'll show you the route we'll be taking on the map."

As he turned to leave, Gatto called out to him. "Hey, Mason, Jonah's part of my gang. What makes you think you can go stealing my people like that?"

Mason swiveled around and came back to the table. He stood over Gatto, his huge frame towering over him. "Because I don't need your damned permission, that's why. Jonah used to be part of Nate's crew, who *I* found. Why the hell shouldn't I take him?"

"Because he's with me now," Gatto protested. "It ain't fair."

Mason eyes narrowed to small black beads. "You got the lodge, don't you? Soon you'll have people begging to join your crew. What the fuck you bitching about?"

Gatto held Mason's gaze a moment, then lowered his eyes. "I suppose you're right. Just don't go taking anymore, okay?" he muttered.

Seeing he'd won the argument, Mason's face relaxed. He slapped Gatto on the shoulder. "Don't worry, it's just me and Murph got a good rap going, that's all. Makes sense he joins me." He looked at Jonah, indicating that he follow him, then turned on his heels and headed out of the dining hall.

Shrugging at Gatto, Jonah stood up. He slung his rifle over his shoulder and followed Mason out of the room.

***

At 8:30 a.m., the three-vehicle convoy drove out of the camp. Gatto's blue Ford, which he'd driven over from his old camp the previous day, led the way. Mason followed in his GMC Canyon. He sat behind the wheel, Doney riding shotgun, while Jonah and a guy named Mike sat in the back seats. In the truck bed, two crew members leaned against either side panel, their rifles pointing outward. Following them, and similarly configured, a third pickup took up the rear.

Halfway down the driveway they passed the main checkpoint, where Mason's guards reversed the eight-wheeler off the road and let them pass. Reaching Cookson Road, they turned left and headed south, deeper into the Cohutta.

A trickle of sweat ran down the side of Jonah's face. A deadly ambush lay somewhere ahead. In the enclosed space of the vehicle with bullets flying everywhere, he was under no illusion that in the next few minutes he might very well end up dead.

They reached the junction of Card Spur Road. To the left, the road ran down to the lakeside by Devil's Point. To the right, it headed toward the Harris Branch. Mason slowed down as Gatto's truck turned right onto Card Spur in front of him.

Jonah gazed anxiously out the window and braced himself, his senses twitching like crazy. Right here was where he would have set up the ambush, at a place where the convoy was forced to slow down. On the radio with Olvan earlier, he hadn't had the chance to ask. Through his window, he'd spotted one of Gatto's crew outside and had hurriedly terminated the call.

His instincts were correct. At that moment, several shots fired off in quick succession.

Crack! Crack! … Crack! Crack!

Mason slammed his foot down on the pedal and tugged hard on the steering wheel. With a screech of its tires, the Canyon swerved sharply onto Card Spur Road.

"Everyone okay?" he shouted as the pickup quickly gathered speed. All three passengers responded affirmatively.

Jonah looked around, confused. None of the truck's windows were damaged. Also, the shots appeared to have come from the right side of the road. Jonah had specifically told Kit Halpern that Mason would be driving the truck. The shooting should have come from the left.

Mason glanced in his rearview mirror. "Dammit! They got Lou and Johnny!" he snarled.

Jonah jerked his head around. Mason's men lay sprawled in the cargo bed, blood streaming from their heads. The shots hadn't missed—they'd taken out two crew members. Back at the junction, the shooting continued. The trailing vehicle had obviously come under fire too.

What the hell is going on? a bewildered Jonah thought to himself. *Why didn't the Bentons taken Mason out?*

Above the sound of the Canyon, he then heard the loud roar of an engine. A moment later, a motorbike appeared on the road. It must have cut out of the forest from somewhere. In a few short seconds, it caught up with them. A man wearing a full-face helmet and a black motorcycle jacket sat hunched behind the handlebars. Behind him, another man held a pistol in his grip.

Now Jonah understood why he'd been instructed to sit behind Mason. With the men in the truck bed eliminated, and the trailing vehicle prevented from following them, Jonah's seat was the last position from which someone could easily fire at the motorbike.

Mason had spotted the bike too. As it roared up to his window, he took a large bite of the steering wheel and jerked it hard. Simultaneously, with his right hand, he pulled the handbrake all the way up. The truck's rear wheels locked and began to slide out across the road. As the car rotated, the motorbike was forced to swerve away or else it would have crashed into the side of the truck. Completing the one-eighty turn, Mason expertly released the handbrake, floored the gas pedal, and the Canyon shot off in the direction they'd just come from.

In a daze, Jonah swiveled his head and looked out the back windscreen to see the motorbike race away. A moment later, it swerved left and disappeared up a forest track.

He turned around again and stared at Mason in disbelief. "How in the name of *jaysus* did you manage that?" It didn't take anything on his part to feign surprise. The last thirty seconds had been straight out of a movie.

"That's the wrong question," Mason replied tightly. "How the hell did the Bentons know we'd be leaving camp right now? Don't tell me they've been sitting around waiting for us for two days."

Doney looked at Mason, his eyes widening. "You're right, boss. Someone must be in on this!"

"Damn straight." Mason slammed his foot on the brakes and the Canyon skidded to a halt in the middle of the road. He pulled out his pistol and jammed it through the gap between the seats, a look of pure rage on his face. "Murph, you better tell me what's going on, or I'll plug you right there where you sit!"

CHAPTER 29

The CVO Breakout tore up the forest trail. Approaching the next bend at breakneck speed, Ralph expertly downshifted, and Cody had to clutch on tightly to the back fender as the Harley's rear wheel skidded in the dirt. Straightening out, Ralph pulled back on the throttle and shifted up through the gears again.

In his mind's eye, Cody reran the sequence of events that had just taken place. He shook his head in frustration. The ambush had been executed to perfection, bar the final act itself, the one that really counted.

At the back of Mason's truck, his two men had been dispatched expertly by Jim Wharton and Clete, the camp's top marksmen, while the trailing vehicle had been fired at head on by Sheriff Rollins and Sam Kirby, preventing it from following Mason.

Given the go-ahead by Walter over the radio, Cody and Ralph, who had been waiting in the forest, drove out onto Card Spur Road and raced up to the Canyon. His pistol raised, Cody had been a split second away from shooting Mason when the bandit had performed an incredible handbrake turn and made a perfect one-eighty on the road.

Cody doubted they would get another chance to take him out. Forewarned now, Mason would take better precautions when he left camp. Though he'd never met Jonah Murphy, Cody feared for him. Mason would be suspicious of how a perfectly-timed ambush like the one they'd just executed could have be done without advance notice. Jonah was likely the first to fall under suspicion.

They reached the end of the trail. Braking hard, Ralph dropped his right shoulder, and the Harley turned onto Baker Creek Road and headed in the direction of the Alaculsy Valley.

Cody tapped Ralph on the shoulder. He slowed and turned his head to one side. "Damn, that was some stunt Mason pulled!" Cody yelled into his helmet. "You ever see anything like that before?"

"Not since my last getaway!" the bank robber yelled back at him. Then he yanked the throttle hard and the Harley picked up speed again, leaving Cody to ponder what he would tell a disappointed war council back at Camp Eastwood.

CHAPTER 30

Jonah stared at the pistol held in Mason's grip. Poked through the front seats, its muzzle was only a couple of feet from his chest.

He gulped hard, a sinking feeling in his stomach. It hadn't taken long for Mason to realize the Bentons must have had inside knowledge. Too much work had gone into the ambush to think otherwise. He'd been rumbled, and now he was going to die.

"Mason, what are yeh talking about? Yeh think I had something to do with this?" Though nothing would save him now, preservation instincts kicked in all the same. Denial was his only option.

From the front passenger seat, Doney stared at him coldly. "Somebody set us up. Makes sense it's the newcomer."

Mason's hard eyes bore into Jonah's. "Murph, answer my questions straight, or I'll blow you to hell. When you told Gatto you'd be joining my crew, how did he take it?"

"Eh?" Jonah replied, taken aback by Mason's line of questioning. It wasn't what he'd been expecting. He recovered fast, though. "To be honest, he was pretty sore about it."

"Sore? Like how?"

"Well, he called you all sorts of names. Said you shouldn't be stealing his people. You know, same thing he told you at the dining hall."

Mason grunted. "Anything else?"

Jonah thought hard. Mason wasn't stupid. He had to play this just right. "I don't know. He sent me to my trailer. While he and the crew talked about it, I guess. I didn't see him again until this morning."

"Boss," Doney cut in, "you really think Gatto's men ambushed us, not the Bentons?"

Mason snorted. "Wake the fuck up, Doney. How the hell could the Bentons have known we'd be leaving camp this morning? It's got to be Gatto."

Doney still looked doubtful, like something wasn't quite right. Jonah prayed he didn't figure it out. "I guess. You think Murph was in on it too?"

"That's what I'm trying to figure out," Mason turned to face Jonah again. "Tell me, any of Gatto's crew got a motorbike?"

A look of surprise came over Jonah's face, as if the thought just occurred to him. "Lenny's got one! He drove it back from their old camp yesterday."

Mason's gaze hardened. "Was it the same one you saw just now?"

Jonah scratched his head. "I'm not sure. It was a big bike...some type of low rider. Sorry, I'm not good on that kind of thing."

That clinched it for Mason. His face grew even darker. "Sonofabitch thought he could kill me and take over my crew. Well, he's got—"

Doney nudged Mason's arm urgently. "Boss! Here comes Gatto now!"

Mason looked past Jonah and through the rear windshield. Jonah turned around too, to see Gatto's blue pickup coming around the bend at speed. Having seen that Mason was no longer following him, he'd turned around.

Mason gritted his teeth. "Here's how we're going to play this. We're going to pretend like we haven't figured this out. Soon as the moment's right, we take the fucker down, got it?"

Sitting beside Jonah, Mike nodded. "Got it, boss."

Ten yards back, the Ford truck pulled to a stop with a screech of its brakes. A moment later, Gatto flung open the driver door and stepped out. Mason gave Jonah one last look. "Here's your opportunity to prove yourself, Murph. Don't blow it."

The four stepped out of the Canyon as Gatto hurried over to them. "Mason, you all right?" he asked anxiously when he reached them.

Mason nodded. "I'm fine. Bastards took out two of my men though."

Gatto spat on the road. "Damn. The Bentons must be closer than we thought. Come on, let's grab some more people and go find them."

Mason stared at the Ford, where Gatto's men sat, watching. "One…two…three…and two more in the bed make five." he counted. "Still leaves three more. Where are they, Gatto?"

Gatto stared at him with a puzzled look. "I left three of my men back at the lodge, if that's what you mean. Murph told me you only needed six of us today."

"True, but if I'd known what was coming, I'd have thought different about it, now wouldn't I?"

Gatto's frown deepened. "Mason, what the fuck you talking about?"

"Three extra men…" Mason mused. "One to take Lou and Johnny out in the truck bed. Another two to do the motorbike hit. It almost worked too, only for the fact I used to be a security driver, trained how to evade and escape."

With a look of horror, Gatto took a step back. "Mason, are you out of your fucking mind? This had nothing to do with me." He turned to Jonah. "Murph, tell him," he pleaded.

Unfortunately for Don Gatto, the time for words was over. So was his life. A stone-faced Jonah pulled out his Glock and shot him twice in the chest. Gatto's knees buckled, and with a short grunt he dropped like a rock.

Before he hit the ground, Jonah took aim again and blasted through the Ford's windshield. A moment later, Mason, Doney, and Mike followed suit. With no time to react, the three men inside the crew cabin were ripped apart in a hail of lead.

Behind, in the load bed, Gatto's two remaining men jumped out and sprinted up the road. They didn't make it far. In seconds, both lay motionless, face down on the tarmac.

Mason raised an arm and called a halt to the shooting. He surveyed the scene a few moments, then said, "Come on. Let's go."

The adrenaline coursing through his body, Jonah flipped his rifle on safety and followed Mason back to the Canyon. All four jumped inside, Mason started the engine, and they were off again. Though still in shock, Jonah felt confident he'd done enough to convince Mason of his loyalty. Every dead crew member gave Colleen and the Bentons a better chance of survival too.

They returned to the junction of Cookson Road to see the trailing pickup wrapped around a tree. As soon as he'd come under attack, the quick-thinking driver had swerved off the road and into the forest to get out of the line of fire. All six men were unharmed, and were in the process of pushing the damaged truck back out onto the road.

Mason ordered Jonah and Mike to dump Lou and Johnny. One by one, the pair lifted the corpses out of truck bed and laid them down in the forest.

When they got back, Mason was waiting impatiently for them. "Come on," he growled. "We still got three more to take care of."

CHAPTER 31

Hunched over the wheel of the Canyon, Mason raced down Cookson Road in the direction of Wasson Lodge. In the back seat, Jonah's mind raced even harder. Having dispatched Gatto and five of his men, Mason now intended killing the remaining three left behind that morning.

One of them was Paul Webb. Jonah felt bad for him. He didn't deserve to die over this. But what was he to do? If he somehow persuaded Mason to spare him, he risked Mason finding out that neither Webb nor the other two had played any part in the ambush earlier. It left Jonah in a quandary, one he had no idea how to resolve. All he could do was see how things played out.

They reached the turn for the lodge. Mason slowed down and pulled into the driveway. He looked around at his men. "Remember what I told you. Once Gatto's men see us, they'll know why we're here. We shoot on sight. Everyone got that?"

"Yeh better believe it," a tight-lipped Jonah replied. "No mercy shown, none expected."

They reached the top of the drive. Mason swung into the lot and pulled up beside a red Toyota truck. "Sloppy," he said, looking around. "They've left no one on guard." He turned in his seat. "Where do you think they are, Murph?"

"Probably waiting for Gatto in the kitchen?" Jonah hoped that was the case. It wouldn't look good if the "ambushers" had gone back to bed once Gatto left that morning. Who went back to bed after botching up an assassination attempt?

The four slid the safeties off their rifles and got out of their vehicle. Leading the way, Jonah strode up the lodge steps and into the lobby, his M-15 at his shoulder. Pausing a moment to listen, he strode down the hall, where the sound of voices in the kitchen could be heard.

As he got closer, someone called out, "That you, Gat? Back already?"

A moment later, Lenny stepped around the corner and into the hallway. He stared at Jonah, then past him at Mason and his two men.

"Murph? What's going on?"

Jonah shot him where he stood, then ran forward. Stepping over Lenny's body, he ran around the corner and into the kitchen. There, Paul Webb and the remaining member of Gatto's crew, a man called Roddy, were rising from the table. A gray cloud of cigarette smoke hung above their heads, and on the table were two coffee mugs.

Wild-eyed, Roddy reached over to where his rifle leaned against the wall. Jonah took aim and shot him in the chest. Arms flailing, Roddy fell backward over his chair and crashed to the floor.

Jonah turned to Webb, who stood transfixed, making no attempt to reach for the holster at his waist. "Murph..." he uttered slowly, as if in a dream. "What the...?"

Jonah aimed his rifle at Webb's chest. His finger trembled on the trigger, unable to bring himself to shoot.

From behind him, a single shot rang out. Brain, bone fragment, and blood sprayed everywhere, and Webb collapsed to the floor.

Mason walked over and stared down at where blood was pooling quickly on the tiled floor. He put two more bullets in Webb's head, then looked back at Jonah. "You killed the first two quick enough. Why not this one, too?"

Ashen-faced, Jonah lowered his rifle. "Pauly had nothing to do with this," he said in almost a whisper. "He was a good geezer."

Mason shrugged indifferently. "Should have told me sooner, then." He clasped Jonah on the shoulder. "Come on. Let's get back to camp."

Wordlessly, Jonah followed him out of the room, sick to the stomach, his heart deader than a two-day-old corpse.

CHAPTER 32

At Camp Eastwood, Walter and Granger were conducting an after-action mission review with the hit team. Although they'd failed in their primary objective, the ambush had yielded a positive outcome nonetheless. Fifteen minutes ago, Jonah had put in a radio call to Kit Halpern on duty at Devil's Point. As well as reassuring him that he was unhurt, he'd informed Halpern on how Mason had killed Don Gatto's entire gang, suspecting them of planning the ambush. Along with Mason's two crew members killed during the attack, it meant that the bandit's numbers had been severely depleted.

"So, what now?" Cody asked, still disappointed he hadn't managed to kill Mason. No blame had been attached to him, however. Only the bandit's quick thinking and extraordinary driving skills had prevented him from being successful.

"The way I see it, we've got two options," Granger replied. "Either we attack Mason, or dig in and wait for him to attack us. It's only a matter of time before he finds this place."

"I say we attack," Cody said. "He's down at least ten men today. That's ten men less to defend the camp."

"Agreed," said Ralph. "We need to do it soon too, before he recruits more people. He's good at that."

"A head on attack will lead to a lot of casualties. Mason's still got the best part of twenty men," Walter said dubiously. He hesitated a moment. "I think I've got a better way of breaking into the camp, but it involves Jonah again."

Olvan shook his head emphatically. "That's not going to happen. Jonah told Kit to arrange for his pick up tonight. He wants out. Can't say I blame him either. He got lucky with Gatto taking the rap today. There's only so much luck a person can count on."

Walter's gaze hardened. "You've got to convince him otherwise, Bert. We've got a spy in the camp, and we need to continue to use that to our advantage. This is war. That's what you do."

CHAPTER 33

As soon as the meeting ended, Cody hurried back to his trailer, anxious to give Emma the news of his adventure. By now, he'd cheered up. In war, not everything went to plan, and he was excited by the latest strategy Walter had presented to the team. How Jonah Murphy might feel about it was another matter.

There was a strange look on Emma's face when he came into the living room to greet her. "What's up?" he asked. "Something happen when I was away?"

"No," Emma replied sullenly, sitting down at the sofa. "Other than I had to hear from somebody secondhand how you went off on a dangerous mission without warning me first."

Cody stared at her blankly. "What are you talking about? You knew all about our plans to hit Mason today."

"Yes, but there's one thing being part of Walter's team, and another trying to execute Mason from the back of a motorcycle. You're lucky you're still alive, you know."

"I'm sorry. We had a last-minute change of plan. I didn't have time to tell you."

"That's not true!" Emma's eyes flashed angrily. "How do you think I know about this? Maya told me. Ralph informed *her* what he was about to do before he left."

"Oh," Cody said feebly. He leaned forward and put his hand on her shoulder.

Emma brushed it away. "At least *her* boyfriend had the courtesy to tell her that he was about to do something dangerous. Something that might get him killed."

"I said I'm sorry." Cody felt his anger rising too. While he probably should have informed Emma about the change in plan and the increased level of danger he'd be under, he had done it for everyone at the camp. He expected to be treated better than this.

"Really? You don't sound it. You think if I had volunteered to do the hit, you wouldn't be angry if I hadn't told you first?"

"You would have never been allowed to," Cody said curtly. "You don't have the skills."

"Oh, you're telling me I'm not good enough to climb on the back of a motorbike and shoot someone through a car window, is that it?" Emma said fiercely.

"There's way more to it than that. You need—"

"Don't tell me what you need, because whatever it is, *you* don't have it. You failed, and Mason got away. So don't act like you're some sort of hero."

Cody stood rigid like a statue, stunned by Emma's words.

"Next time Camp Eastwood needs a volunteer to do something dangerous," she continued, "guess what? It's going to be me. Ever since vPox took away everyone I loved, I live one day at a time. You're not the only risk taker around here."

Rising from the couch, she brushed past him and stormed out of the cabin, leaving an open-mouthed Cody in her wake. He shook his head and sighed. It was one of these days where absolutely nothing had gone according to plan.

CHAPTER 34

Emma and Greta sat on folding stools outside what the camp now called the "med center". It was late afternoon and the two, dressed in t-shirts and shorts, were sunning themselves, their legs stretched out in front of them.

Greta had just informed Emma how a strike force comprised of the entire Eastwood and Benton groups would attack Mason the following morning at dawn. Both Walter and Granger felt that, given the limited fighting experience of many in the two groups, it would be easier to plan than a night assault.

Outside of the war council, Greta had been the first to learn of the plan. That didn't surprise Emma, given her relationship with Walter.

"Anyway, I only learned about it a few minutes ago," Greta finished up by saying. "Expect an announcement on it soon."

Emma frowned. "How come neither you nor me were involved in the planning?" she asked, still smarting over Cody's attitude toward her that morning. "Don't you think the women should have had a say in the decision too? I mean, we're all in this together."

Greta shook her head. "Emma, it's not like that. The war council was assembled based on people's previous military or weapons experience. It doesn't exclude women at all. In fact, Mary Sadowski is on it. I gather from Walter that her views are taken very seriously, too."

"Oh...I didn't know that." Emma felt a little foolish. Cody hadn't never mentioned that to her. "Do you know who's going to be involved in the attack?"

"No idea. Presumably everyone who's fit and able. Don't worry, we'll all be assigned our roles soon enough."

A determined look came over Emma's face. "Well, I'm fit and able. And I've become a damned good shot lately too." What she said was true. Under Cody's tutelage, her firearm skills now excelled many of the men at the camp.

Greta smiled, looking amused by Emma's obtuse behavior. "Hey, you'll be with me, girl." She jerked her thumb back at the trailer. "We'll be setting up the med center at Devil's Point, ready to treat any casualties. Remember what I told you about the 'golden hour'? It's vital we're at hand somewhere close by."

Greta was referring to the time period in emergency medicine where, during the first sixty minutes, a patient stood the highest likelihood of survival following any traumatic injury. After that, it tended to fall off dramatically.

Emma shook her head. "I should be involved in the attack. We need everyone who can shoot straight to fight Mason. I'm sure you can cope on your own."

"No, Emma," Greta said sharply. "I need you with me to treat the wounded tomorrow. It's the reason I trained you in the first place. What the hell's gotten into you?"

Over the past week, Greta had been familiarizing Emma with what to expect in a triage situation involving multiple casualties. She clearly expected Emma to be by her side during the battle.

Emma sighed, irritated by how her pride had stupidly placed her on the wrong side of this argument. However, she had no intention of backing down. "Greta, I really should be with the strike force. If Cody thinks he's the only one who can go taking all the risks while…" She broke off, realizing how stupid she was sounding. "Oh, never mind."

Greta stared at her curiously. "Tell me, what's eating you?" she asked, her tone softening a little.

Emma hesitated a moment, then went on to tell Greta about her argument with Cody earlier that day and how annoyed she'd been by his attitude.

Greta listened carefully to what she had to say. When Emma finished, she shrugged. "I wouldn't be too hard on Cody. He's young and headstrong, just like you. He's also a natural soldier, and a great marksman too, from what I've been told. When it comes to things like war, men and women *are* different, you know."

Puzzled by Greta's remark, Emma was about to question her further when she caught sight of Colleen walking through the farmhouse's front garden and into the field where the med center was parked. The Irishwoman had a dry sense of humor that Emma appreciated, and the two had become increasingly more friendly since she'd arrived at the camp.

After greeting her, she indicated for Colleen to grab one of the spare foldout stools leaning against the trailer and join them. "You look worried," she said, observing Colleen carefully after she sat down. "What gives? Is it something to do with Jonah?"

Colleen nodded. "Bert promised me that after the ambush this morning, he'd be coming straight back here, that it would be too dangerous for him to stay with Mason afterward. Now he's telling me Jonah needs to stay one more day, that he's got something important to do tomorrow. I'm not stupid, I know exactly what that means. They want him to do something dangerous again." She sighed. "I feel so guilty doing nothing but defensive drills around here while he's over there taking all the risks."

Emma and Greta exchanged glances. "Colleen, there's a plan underway to attack Mason tomorrow, an all-out assault," Emma told her. "I'm guessing that's the reason he needs to remain one more night."

Colleen's eyebrows shot up in surprise. "Bert never said anything to me about that."

"It's not official yet," Greta told her. "I only heard about it a few minutes ago."

A determined glint came into Colleen's eye. "Well I won't stand by twiddling my thumbs tomorrow, that's for sure. I'll go see Mary later and make sure I'm assigned to her QRF squad."

"Attagirl," Greta said approvingly.

Emma stared at her indignantly. "If Colleen is going to be involved in the attack, I don't see why I—"

"*Emma!*" Greta snapped. "What did I tell you about me needing you tomorrow?"

There was a determined glint in Emma's eye now too. "I got an idea about that. I think I know just the person to help you. Someone far more experienced than me."

CHAPTER 35

The rest of the day had gone by in a blur as Jonah struggled to come to terms with the morning's carnage.

After leaving the bloody scene at the lodge, Mason returned to camp, where he set about arranging a second convoy. He was hell-bent on finding the remnants of the Benton group that day, and thirty minutes later, they were back on the road again.

The butchery of Gatto and his crew appeared to have little effect on the bandit. If anything, it had only served to increase his appetite for violence. For Jonah, it had the opposite effect. It sickened him to his very core, particularly the death of Paul Webb. All day long, the gruesome image of Webb's brains dripping down the side of his head flashed in his mind, no matter how hard he tried to stop it.

A terrible guilt hung over him. Although he hadn't pulled the trigger himself, he'd done nothing to prevent Webb's death. Deep in his heart, he knew he could have done more to save the man. The one thing that consoled him was the knowledge that in saving Webb, he would have put his own life at risk. For Colleen's sake, he couldn't allow that. He had to do everything in his power to come out of this situation alive.

The convoy spent several hours scouring Lake Ocoee's southern shoreline, following the forest service road all the way to its eastern tip, where it connected with Highway 64. Whether deliberate or not, Olvan hadn't disclosed the whereabouts of Camp Eastwood to Jonah, and it proved to be a nerve-racking trip. At every survivor camp they stumbled across, he held his breath, his right hand down at his waist. If they encountered the Bentons, Jonah planned to kill Mason first, then take Doney and Mike out. With Lou and Johnny's replacements sitting behind him in the truck bed, however, he doubted he would survive much longer beyond that.

To his relief, there was no sign of the Bentons at any of the lakeside camps they visited, nor along the myriad forest trails that crisscrossed the lake's hinterland. By late afternoon, they returned to camp where he finally got a chance to get away from Mason.

He went back to Chickasaw, pleased to see that the cabin was still unoccupied. Being so far from the square, it appeared no one wanted to take it. He rested a few minutes, then headed around the back of the cabin and into the woods. Other than for a rushed twenty second call to Kit while Mason had been reorganizing the convoy earlier, this would be his first chance to talk properly since the ambush. There was only one subject on his mind. He wanted out. He had done his duty. Now he needed to get back to Colleen.

He'd already planned the first thing he would tell her when they met, something he'd been thinking about all day. This feud between Mason and the Bentons wasn't going to end anytime soon. Tomorrow, the two of them would leave the Cohutta and head for the coast like they'd originally planned. The more he thought about it, the more he knew it was the right thing to do. This wasn't their fight. He couldn't put Colleen in any more danger.

Reaching the birch tree where he'd made his call the previous afternoon, he powered up his radio. "Bert? Kit?" he whispered. "Who's there, over?"

At Devil's Point, Bert Olvan was on duty and answered his call right away. Dispensing with any formalities, Jonah got straight to business. "Right Bert, like I told Kit this morning, I'm out of here. Where and when are yis going to pick me up? Over."

There was a brief hesitation before Olvan responded. *"We're not ready to pull you out yet, Jonah. There's one more thing we need you to do. I know it's a big ask, but we're really depending on you. Over."*

Jonah was unable to believe what he was hearing. He jabbed his finger down on the Talk button. Barely containing his anger, he said, "Bert, the deal was that once I set up your ambush, you'd get me out of here. I kept me side of the bargain, time for you to keep yours, over." Releasing the button, he pressed the radio set up close to his ear.

Across the airwaves, Olvan's tone became more urgent. *"Listen to me, Jonah. We have a plan drawn up to take back the camp tomorrow. It's a full-scale attack involving Walter and his people. We need you to help ensure its success. It's a little risky, I can't deny that, but it's going to help save many lives, over."*

"A little risky?" Jonah almost yelped. "Bert, have yeh any idea what I went through today? Me nerves are shot to hell!"

"You did great today, truly," Olvan said soothingly. *"Tomorrow you'll see Colleen, I promise you. But you're there on the inside, and we need—"*

"Enough, Bert!" There was a hard edge to Jonah's voice now. "I'm done here. Tell me where yer picking me up. If I don't get back to Colleen today, she'll go through me for a shortcut."

Olvan had an apologetic tone when he spoke. *"Thing is…Colleen will be involved in tomorrow's operation. She insists on doing her part. See, by helping us, you'll be helping her too. Can't you see that? Over."*

Jonah's entire body stiffened. The Bentons had deliberately involved Colleen in this to ensure his cooperation, he was sure of it. Bert knew the type of person she was: that if asked, she would agree to join in the attack on the camp.

An ice-cold fury surged through his veins. "You've no right to use my wife like this!" he hissed. "Keep her out of it, or so help me God, I'll walk out of here right now and kill the bleedin' lot of yis. I've enough blood on me hands now, it makes no difference to me."

"Jonah! It's not what you think! Emma and Greta will be involved tomorrow too. It's what being part of this group entails. One thing I can tell you is that your help will greatly improve both hers and everyone else's chances of surviving. What do you say, over?"

Jonah wrestled with his emotions. All day long he'd been waiting to make contact with the Bentons so he could arrange to get the hell away from Mason. Instead, it appeared he was being coerced into yet another dangerous situation. The Bentons had stitched him up like a little kipper.

"Will you do this for us?" Olvan pressed.

"Yeah, I'll do it," Jonah said, his voice grating harshly. "But I tell yeh this, soon as this is done, me and Colleen are leaving the Cohutta. I'll have nothing more to do with the Bentons. I'm sick of yis."

"I hope you feel different about this tomorrow," Olvan replied gently. *"Right now, it's important you listen to me very carefully. The success of tomorrow's operation depends entirely on you."*

CHAPTER 36

Early that evening, Walter was in the bunkhouse of the travel trailer he shared with Pete, packing his things. He'd been living in the nineteen-foot Venture Sonic Lite for over a week, ever since he'd donated his own trailer to Greta when the newly-formed Eastwood group departed from Wasson Lodge. Of course, things had been a little different back then. He and Greta had barely known each other.

He removed the last of his clothes from the closet and placed them in his backpack. "Well, that's it, partner," he said, zipping it up. "Time for this rambler to move on. I need to go find me a pallet on someone else's floor."

"You won't be sleeping on no floor but in the arms of a beautiful woman," Pete replied a little wistfully, watching his friend from the hallway. "Wish I knew what it took to find somebody like that."

Walter grinned. "Here's a tip. Lend your trailer to the next pretty woman that shows up at camp. Wait a few days, then insist on moving in with her. Worked for me."

The previous night he and Greta had talked into the early hours of the morning, and decided it didn't make sense for him to continue bunking with Pete, especially seeing as everyone at the camp now knew of their relationship.

Although they hadn't been together long, Walter was surprised by how good he felt about the decision.

Attractive and highly intelligent, Greta had a set of moral values that he'd come to respect. And despite her haughty nature that was at times imperious even, in private she was surprisingly warm and affectionate. Walter liked that. In fact, he liked it a lot, and the two realized that in these uncertain times, they had to make the most of their lives. If things worked out, great. If not, so be it.

He picked up his pack and threw it over one shoulder, then pointed to the remainder of his gear he'd stowed neatly in one corner. "I'll have the porters pick up the rest of my things in the morning."

Pete laughed. "If I haven't sold them first, that is." He escorted Walter to the door, looking at him awkwardly as he pushed it open for him. "Guess I'll see you around. It's not like you're going far. Can't be all of five hundred yards."

"If that. And you'll see me soon enough. Tomorrow morning we'll be heading out of camp bright and early. There's a certain party down by the lake we're both invited to, remember?"

With those parting words, Walter grabbed the rifle he'd left by the doorway and, laden down with his gear, trod carefully down the trailer steps.

Instead of going through the front garden to get to Greta's trailer, he headed around the back of house, walking parallel to the side fence. He felt awkward carrying his gear, and preferred as few people as possible saw him as he made his move to Greta's.

Reaching the corner, he walked by the back-garden fence, and a few minutes later entered the far field where Greta's trailer sat parked in the middle. Fifty yards away, under a stand of apple trees, three tents had been pitched belonging to their new recruits Marcie, Simone, Jenny, Laura, and Billy.

Thankfully, only Billy was around. He sat on a blanket outside his tent reading a large hardback book. Seeing him coming, the boy gave him a solemn wave.

Walter waved back at him. "What you reading there?"

Billy raised the book to reveal a cover with plenty of green on it. *"The Resilient Farm and Homestead!"* he yelled back. "It was one of my Dad's favorite books."

Walter nodded appreciatively. "Resilient, huh? I like that. Keep on reading."

He reached the trailer and came up the steps. Knocking lightly on the door, he pulled it open. "Honey...I'm home!" he called out, trying to dislodge a sudden nervousness that had come over him.

He peered down the hallway to see Greta poke her head out of the kitchen area. In one hand she held a large box of bandages, which she set down, then walked quickly over to him. "Welcome home, darling. How was your trip?" Laughing, she flung her arms around his neck and kissed him hard on the lips.

"Pretty uneventful. Traffic was light," he replied once she'd let him go of him, feeling his awkwardness melt away. "Where shall I put my things?"

Pulling away from him, Greta wagged her finger and headed toward the bedroom. "Follow me. I have some closet space all set up for you. Once you've settled in, we need to talk. There's been a change in staffing for the med center tomorrow. Don't worry, nothing that will cause any problems"

"All right. After that we should relax. Tomorrow is going to be one hell of a day." Walter grinned. "I got something in mind that ought to help us loosen up."

CHAPTER 37

Early the following morning, hands in his pockets, Jonah strolled down the camp driveway in the direction of the main checkpoint, previously known to the Bentons as Papa Three. It was 6:25 a.m. and a pink-tinged dawn was breaking in the skies above him, heralding the arrival of yet another beautiful day.

Another day in paradise, he thought to himself grimly. *Shame I'm about to go through hell again.*

To anyone who might be watching, Jonah appeared relaxed, his shoulders slack, his gait nonchalant. But that was just a show. On closer observation, an onlooker would detect how drawn his face was, the corners of his mouth tucked down in a stiff grimace. For once, none of this was due to a hangover either. The previous evening, Mason had opted for a quiet night in with Tania, and Jonah had been grateful to stay alone in his cabin. With what was coming up, he hadn't wanted to risk betraying to anyone just how anxious he felt.

He walked around the bend to see the eight wheeler parked across the driveway. Four of Mason's men were on duty. Two sat on stools placed on either side of the truck, while two more sat up on the flatbed, smoking cigarettes. All four carried pistols by their waists, their semi-automatic rifles resting against the side of the truck. Jonah took a gulp of air and steadied his nerves.

"How's it going, lads?" he said affably as he approached them. "Mind if I join yis?"

"What brings you here so early?" a man named Sal, one of the two sitting atop the flatbed, responded gruffly. He was a hatchet-faced man with a sallow complexion and spiky black hair who shared the same cold-eyed demeanor as most of Mason's crew. "Changeover's not until eight."

Jonah grinned. "I woke up early and couldn't get back to sleep. Thought I'd come down and make sure yis were all awake."

Sal gave him a look. "Listen, Murph, we don't want to hear any of your bullshit stories. All that Irish baloney don't truck with us." He turned to the guard sitting next to him who leaned against the back of the cabin, one leg dangling over the side. "You know something, Howie? Murph reminds me a little of Russ." He took a last drag from his cigarette and flicked the butt into the forest. "A mouthy fucker who spends the whole time brown-nosing Mason. What do you think?"

An unpleasant smile came over Howie's face. "Now that you mention it, Russ was kinda mouthy too, all right." He looked at Jonah. "Before your time, Murph. Let's just say, things didn't turn out so good for him." Sal and the two guards sitting at each end of the truck broke out into wry chuckles. "Us boys were *real* sorry about it too."

Actually, Jonah knew quite a lot about Russ. He'd witnessed his execution the other morning. He stretched his hands out lazily in the air and yawned. "Russ, you say? That the weaselly little geezer who peed his pants when the Bentons executed his ass?"

Sal's face immediately hardened. "Who the hell told you that? Mason?"

Jonah looked around. Something should have happened by now. Placing his hands in the air had been the agreed signal to commence the attack. He realized that standing so close in front of Sal, perhaps the spotter in the forest couldn't see him. He stepped back a few feet. "Eh…yeah. Must have heard it from Mason. Can't think who else," he mumbled, then raised both arms again and awkwardly mimicked a second yawn.

Sal and Howie exchanged puzzled glances. "The fuck you acting so weird for, Murph?" Sal asked suspiciously. "Are you—"

He broke off as the thin crack of a rifle shot rang in the air. The back of Howie's head exploded, and pieces of bone fragment and blood sprayed across the side of Sal's face. "Holy fuck!" he yelled, jumping down off the side of the truck. A moment later, Howie's body teetered over and landed beside him with a soft thud.

Ignoring his dead companion, Sal peered anxiously over the top of the flatbed down the driveway. Jonah whipped out his Glock and crouched alongside him, while the two other guards sprung to their feet and grabbed their AR-15s. All four warily scanned the area in front of them.

To either side, the reports from more firearms broke out in the forest. Along the perimeter, Mason's men called out to each other before returning fire at the intruders.

Sal reached into his pocket and pulled out a two-way radio. "Better call Mason," he said. "Looks like the Bentons want to fuck with us."

"Got that in one, Sal," Jonah said quietly, squatting beside him. "Guess what? Payback is a bitch."

Sal glanced over at him. His eyes widened as Jonah's Glock turned to point at him. Before he could react, Jonah squeezed the trigger and planted a 9 mm slug dead center in his forehead. With a look of astonishment still registered on his face, Sal keeled over.

Swiveling to the right, Jonah shot the guard squatting by the truck's tailgate. Only ten feet away it was an easy shot, and he buried two more .45 ACP rounds in the side of the man's head.

The remaining guard, positioned by the truck's front wheel, was a young man named Ricky. In his early twenties, Jonah had talked to him briefly at the square the night Mason stormed the camp. Though perhaps a little dull, he didn't appear to be the same caliber of cold-hearted killer as the rest of Mason's crew.

Clearly panicked, Ricky leapt to his feet. Making no attempt to shoot at Jonah, he ran around the front of the truck and sprinted toward the forest.

Jonah chased after him and popped off two shots. One caught Ricky in the thigh. He staggered, then fell to the ground. Jonah lowered his pistol. He didn't have the heart to finish him off. The young man scrambled to his feet and hobbled into the forest. A moment later, he disappeared behind the tree line.

Jonah turned on his heels and raced back to the truck. His job wasn't finished yet.

***

Mason woke up with a jerk to the sound of a single gunshot. He sat up in bed and checked his watch. It was 6:35 a.m. A moment later, sporadic gunfire broke out. It sounded like it came from along the camp's main perimeter.

He grabbed his radio from off the bedstand and keyed the mic. "Mason to perimeter. What's going on up there, over?"

Almost as soon as he released the Talk button, one of his men came over the channel. *"Mason, this is Curtis. We got a couple of people shooting at us in the north forest. Nothing we can't handle, over."*

"Copy that," Mason replied, breathing a little easier. A moment later, he received a similar report from another senior guard named Joey at the south forest post. It appeared that the Bentons were engaging his men, but nothing that resembled a full out assault. With his men occupying the well-constructed posts the Bentons had kindly built for him, he was confident that any attack would be easily repelled. Or perhaps this was a fakeout, he thought in sudden realization, and they were planning their main invasion from the beach. If that was the case, he was ready for that too.

Instructing Tania, who by now had woken up, to go back to sleep, he got out of bed. He put on his shorts, then reached over to a cabinet drawer and pulled out a fresh t-shirt and socks. After lacing his boots, he strapped on his holster, grabbed his rifle, and exited the trailer.

His men were likewise emerging from their trailers and nearby cabins. A sleepy Doney skipped hurriedly over to him, buckling his gun holster as he walked. "Everything okay, boss?"

Mason nodded. He took out his radio again. "Sal, where the hell are you?" he yelled impatiently. No one had reported back from the main checkpoint yet.

Only a low level static hum answered him for reply.

"That's not like Sal," Doney said, frowning. "Maybe his battery is dead."

About to try and raise him once more, Mason's radio crackled to life. It was Curtis, sounding a lot more urgent this time. "*Mason, Ricky's just shown up at my post. He says that Murph's gone crazy! He killed Sal and everyone else at the main checkpoint. What do you want me to do, over?*"

Mason looked at Doney, his senses reeling. In what felt like slow motion, he understood that somehow the Irishman was involved with the Bentons. In the next moment came an even worse realization. The Bentons had no intention of making a lakeside assault. He knew exactly what they were going to do.

***

When he got to the eight-wheeler, Jonah stepped over Howie's body and yanked open the driver's door. He climbed inside the cabin, and was relieved to find the key in the ignition. It would save time searching four dead bodies. He cranked the heavy diesel engine, then reversed back until the truck's front wheels were fully off the driveway.

Job done, he reached into his pocket and pulled out his radio. "Bert, this is Jonah. *Blitzkrieg* is a go!" he said breathlessly, giving the signal Olvan had issued him to indicate that the driveway was clear. "Repeat…*Blitzkrieg* is a go!"

"*Roger that, Jonah*," an unfamiliar voice responded moments later. "*This is Walter. We're on our way. Over and out.*"

Jonah killed the engine and clambered out of the cabin. After dragging the three dead men to the side of the road, he picked up Sal's AR-15. If Mason's men arrived before the Bentons, he would need it.

He waited anxiously, crouched behind the truck's left front wheel. In the forest to either side of him, the sharp crackle of gunfire continued. The Bentons had positioned shooters there to occupy Mason's men while he took out the checkpoint.

After what seemed like an interminable amount of time, which in reality was no more than a minute, the sound of engines roared up the drive from the direction of Cookson Road. The next moment, a white pickup truck tore around the bend. A dark blue truck followed right behind, then another truck. He counted five in total, each crammed with armed men.

According to Bert, the plan was to make a daring assault directly down the camp's main driveway. With Jonah's previous intel that Mason hadn't posted any guards along the roadside behind the Papa Three checkpoint, it left a clear route all the way to the parking lot. With the element of surprise, Olvan had assured him they would quickly take back the camp. Knowing Mason, Jonah wasn't quite so confident.

When the first pickup reached him, Jonah walked out onto the driveway and waved it down. In the load bed, several men crouched on either side of the bed panel, their rifles pointing outward. Behind the wheel was a black man with cropped hair and a short goatee beard. He stared past Jonah at the three dead men lying along the side of the road.

"Nice work," he said, then jerked a thumb toward the back of the truck. "Get in. Somebody wants to say hello to you."

Jonah turned his head to see a girl in combat fatigues leaning over the truck panel. Pretty, with short, wavy blonde hair, she smiled at him. A giddy feeling swept over Jonah. He broke out into a huge smile, then took two strides and hopped over the side of the truck.

Crouched down, he and Colleen hugged tightly. Overjoyed to see her, all the words Jonah had been saving up to tell her came out in one babbling, incoherent rant. Luckily for Colleen, the truck took off again with a jerk and she broke off their embrace. She looked him firmly in the eye. "Save the romance until later. We're about to *blitzkrieg* the living daylights out of Mason."

Jonah grinned back at her. "*Achtung* baby! I love it when you talk dirty like that!"

CHAPTER 38

Walter raced up Camp Benton's driveway, checking his mirror constantly to make sure the rest of the convoy followed close behind. Beside him in the passenger seat, Cody sat with his SR-556 Ruger carbine poked out the window, watching the side of the forest warily for any movement.

So far, everything had gone according to plan. Jonah had performed his part to a T. Now time was imperative. They needed to reach the Ring before Mason rallied his men.

The previous afternoon, Walter and Ned Granger had drawn up their ambitious plan. Thanks to Jonah's intel, they knew the sandbag positions along the side of the driveway were unmanned. Mason had opted to deploy extra men across his perimeter instead. Now they had every chance of bypassing his defenses and make a lightning strike at the very heart of the camp.

"Let's *Blitzkrieg* the mothers," Ralph had said, nodding approvingly on hearing the plan. Yet again, the bank robber had nailed the codename for the operation.

The Tundra burst into the parking lot. Walter blew a sigh of relief to see that the western section of the Ring lay undefended. What had been originally designed as a defensive position would provide cover for the combined Eastwood and Benton forces to launch their attack.

He raced across the graveled lot, while behind him the rest of the assault team spread out to their designated positions. To his right, a truck carrying Mary's QRF squad flew past him, heading toward the south side of the Ring. The plan was to command two fields of fire into the square, pinning Mason down and making it difficult for him to organize his defenses.

They arrived with seconds to spare. Coming up the main path from the square, a handful of Mason's men jogged toward the parking lot, rifles in hand. Seeing the Bentons swarm the area, they slowed down, unsure whether to continue forward or not. Their indecision didn't last long. From the back of the Tundra, Walter's men opened fire and sent them running back toward the square.

He jerked the wheel of the Tundra and screeched to a halt parallel to the four-foot-high line of sandbags. His team spilled out of the truck and took up positions behind the Ring. Squatting behind the sandbags, they rested their rifles over the tops and began firing through the gaps between the cabins that faced into the square.

Walter grabbed his rifle and threw open his door. "Let's go, kid!" he yelled. "Time to kick Mason's ass!"

***

From behind a U-shaped defensive post outside what had been the YMCA's infirmary, Mason watched with concern as his men ran back into the square in disarray. Minutes ago, he'd dispatched them with instructions to take up positions behind the sandbags lining the back of the parking lot. They'd arrived too late, and had been sent scurrying back with their tails between their legs.

As they jogged over to him, a fusillade of rifle fire opened up, this time from the south side of the square. The Bentons had opened up another line of attack. The vicious crossfire caught a couple of his men, one falling to the ground in a heap. The rest scattered around the square, racing to get into cover.

A short, ferocious firefight ensued. Mason's men fought hard, but with no clear strategy on how to repel the Bentons, his crew were being run ragged, exposed to rifle fire anytime they poked their noses from out of cover.

"Boss, we need to move!" Doney shouted to him above the din. "They're cutting us to pieces here!"

Mason thought hard. His best option was to pull back to the east side of the square and regroup. From there, he would lead a group of men and try to outflank the main Benton force at the parking lot.

He yelled out the order to retreat. Moments later, his men raced across the square as a hail of deadly metal whistled around them. Leading the way, Mason couldn't help but think how, three nights ago, the shoe had been on the other foot when he and his men had pursued the Bentons in the opposite direction as they fled down to the lake shore.

Following right behind Mason was Doney. Since the fighting began, he had stood no more than three feet from him, shielding him as much as possible any time they broke from cover. As always, his bodyguard was loyal to the core.

Reaching the far end of the square, Mason ducked around the back of a stack of sandbags and threw himself to the ground. Moments later, the rest of his men took up similar positions and began firing back at the Bentons.

Mason pulled out his radio. "Curtis, Joey, where are you?" he yelled breathlessly into the tiny mouthpiece. A few minutes prior, he'd instructed his men posted along the forest perimeter to combine under Curtis and Joey's command and return immediately. It was pointless them guarding it anymore. "Have you reached the lot yet, over?" His plan was for the two groups to attack the Bentons from behind while he cut through the forest and attacked their left flank.

He had to wait several seconds before Curtis answered. "*We're here, boss. What's the plan, over?*"

"Get ready to attack. I'll head through the east forest and hit them from the side, over"

"Mason, you'll never make it. They just sent a group in there. There's at least eight of them!"

Mason cursed out loud. It seemed like every decision he took had been anticipated by the Bentons. "Hold your position. We'll make it, one way or the other." If Mason couldn't repel the main Benton force, it was game over.

"Can't do that. They've spotted us. We have to pull back."

Over the radio, Mason heard the sharp crackle of gunfire in the background. "There's plenty of forest to hide in," he barked into the handset. "Move to another position and wait for me."

"Sorry boss, can't do that. The Bentons are swarming the place. We got to get out of here."

Mason couldn't believe his ears. Curtis was cutting out on him. There was no word from Joey either, and Mason guessed he had already split.

"Curtis!" he screamed into the mic. "Hold your position or I'll strap you to a tree and cut your balls off when I find you, do you hear me?"

A hiss of static squelched back at him for reply.

"Chickenshit bastard!" Doney spat out, squatting beside him.

Mason peeked his head over the sandbags to see the Bentons flooding into the square, taking up the positions they'd just abandoned. At that moment, he knew the game was up.

CHAPTER 39

Vaulting over the line of sandbags that comprised the Ring, Walter's squad raced across twenty yards of open ground, then down the footpaths between the cabins before pouring into the square. They spread out and took up positions behind the defensive posts Mason and his men had just vacated.

Running alongside Emma, Cody pointed to a large U-shaped stack of sandbags outside a cabin where a Red Cross sign hung above the door. The two sprinted over and ducked behind it to the sound of rifle fire crashing above their heads.

When he'd gotten out of the Tundra earlier, Cody had run around the back of the truck just as Emma clambered down off the tailgate. Since then, he hadn't let her stray more than a few feet from him. While he dearly wished she was somewhere safer, he knew that if anyone was to blame for her insistence on fighting that day, it was him. Marcie, a trained nurse, was in Emma's place with Greta at the medical trailer parked at Devil's Point.

He rested the barrel of his Ruger SR across the top of the parapet and stared down the iron sights to where Mason and his men had taken up positions on the far side of the square.

From the southeast corner, a barrage of semi-automatic rifle fire opened up. Having moved stealthily east along the back of the cabins, Mary's QRF squad had successfully established a flanking position on Mason's left.

Cody grinned. So far, everything was going according to plan. Aided by the intel from Jonah Murphy, Granger and Walter knew the exact layout of the camp's defenses. Right now, a team led by Ralph was traversing the east forest to come up behind Mason's position. The net was quickly closing in on the bandit.

Caught once more between two interlocking fields of fire, Mason's men quickly capitulated. Retreating from their positions, they ran down the narrow pathways between the cabins and headed east toward the river. Cody scanned the area, but saw no sign of Mason. Maybe he'd already left. Perhaps it was why his men had given up so easily.

He stood up. "Come on!" he yelled excitedly to Emma. Along with the rest of Walter's squad, the two ran out from their positions and began firing at the fleeing group. Mason's time was up. Cody was certain of it.

***

Moments before, Mason had come to the same conclusion. Only one option remained open to him. Crouched behind the sandbags while bullets thudded into them relentlessly with a hard *thwap*ing sound, he yelled in Doney's ear, "I'm going to fetch Tania. Then we head to the lake."

On their first day at the camp, the two men had hidden a skiff in a small cove along the north shore. It was loaded with emergency food and water, extra clothing, weapons, and ammunition. Enough for the three to survive for a week. It had simply been a practical precaution. Mason had never dreamed he would need to use it.

Doney nodded, a grim look of determination on his face. "Go, boss. I'll be right behind you."

Tapping him on the shoulder, Mason sprinted between two cabins and headed for the bridge that would take him to the field where his trailer was parked.

Two minutes later, flagging and out of breath, he stumbled across the wooden bridge with heavy footsteps. Reaching the far side, he looked back to see that Doney had left the square and was on his way too.

When he arrived at the field, he jogged over to his trailer, bellowing Tania's name as he ran. The door opened and she tentatively poked her head out. "I hear shooting everywhere," she said anxiously. "Is everything okay?"

"Come on. We got to go!" Mason shouted. "The Bentons have taken over the camp."

Tania put a hand up to her mouth. "My God!" she gasped, then rushed down the steps. Mason grabbed her hand and the two raced around the back of the trailer in the direction of the north headland.

Seeing him retreat from the square, Mason's men had soon followed suit. Abandoning their positions, they scattered in all directions. Some headed for the bridge, others into the stream below and up the other side. All shared one thing in common. Blind panic. Behind them, in full pursuit, the Bentons fired at them as they ran.

Ten yards from the edge of the forest and gasping for breath, Mason turned his head to check on Doney. Halfway across the field, his bodyguard moved awkwardly. Mason could tell he'd been shot. "Come on, Doney!" he yelled, gesturing to him urgently. "Keep going!"

A few seconds later, he and Tania reached the forest. Mason ducked around the back of a tree and pulled Tania in after him. Peering out, he saw Doney practically dragging himself across the field. Behind him, a group of Benton men had reached Mason's trailer. Mason stepped out from behind the tree, raised his Heckler to his shoulder and fired at them in short, controlled bursts.

195

A lanky young man with shoulder-length hair and a woman around the same age both dropped to their knees. The man raised his rifle to his shoulder, took aim, and a single shot rang out. A hundred yards away, Doney's two arms spread out wide as he fell face forward to the ground.

Behind the tree, Tania threw both hands to her face. "Doney!" she shrieked. "No!"

Doney remained motionless on the ground.

Mason gritted his teeth, then grabbed Tania by the arm. "Come on!" he yelled. "We got to get out of here!"

***

Cody lowered his rifle and stood to his feet. At the forest edge, Mason fled, pulling his girl along. A girl Cody didn't much care for. It was the same petite blonde who'd stood beside Mason at the Chevron station in Knoxville two weeks ago.

Ahead of him, Ralph, Clete, and four Benton men ran across the field. When they reached the forest, they disappeared from view. A minute later, Ralph and Clete reemerged again. It appeared Mason had lost them in the woods. The Benton men hadn't given up though. Given all that had transpired between the two groups, Cody wasn't surprised.

Around the camp, the shooting petered out, then ended. What remained of Mason's crew had either fled or surrendered. Many were wounded, and corpses littered the area. Walter and Granger's plan had worked perfectly. They had taken back the camp.

The two ex-cons sauntered back across the field, their rifles slung over their shoulders.

"Nice shooting, kid. You dropped that dude stone-cold dead," Clete said when they reached him, pointing back to where Mason's companion lay, face first in the grass. He looked to either side of him, surveying the scene. "Well, that's all for now, folks. Show's over. That didn't take long, did it?"

"*Blitzkrieg*, baby," Emma replied, glancing at Ralph, a big smile on her face.

"Helluva name, helluva plan," Cody said, grinning from ear to ear. He grabbed Emma by the arm and, walking lockstep, the four headed back toward the square.

CHAPTER 40

Mason crept through the trees with Tania in tow. The shooting had stopped, and he knew the battle for the camp was over. Behind him, he heard voices in the forest, calling out urgently to each other. He quickened his stride. He had to get off the headland right away or he was a dead man.

As he walked, his rifle held in his grip, he thought about Murph. Up until now, he'd had no time to process what had occurred at the checkpoint. Why had the Irishman betrayed him like that? It made no sense. One thing was for sure, Murph hadn't gone crazy. His actions were part of a coordinated attack that had allowed the Bentons to break into the camp. Had Murph made some secret pact with them over the past few days? He shook his head in frustration, resigning himself to the fact that he would probably never know the Irishman's motivation.

He spotted the blue waters of the lake through the trees, and put the thought out of his mind. Moments later, he reached the shoreline and poked his head out cautiously to get his bearings.

A hundred yards north, he spotted the crooked pine tree leaning out over the water at an angle and heaved a sigh of relief. It was the visual marker indicating where he and Doney had hidden the skiff around the next point.

He ducked back into the forest and gestured for Tania to follow him, and the two trekked north parallel to the shoreline.

A few minutes later, Mason located the skiff hidden under a large clump of bushes. "Hold this," he whispered to Tania, handing her his rifle, then, stooping over, he grabbed the skiff by the bow rail and began dragging it toward the beach.

Though flat-bottomed and only ten feet long, laden with supplies and its twenty horsepower motor attached, the boat must have weighed over three hundred pounds. Without Doney to help, it was tough going dragging it along the forest floor, even for a huge man such as himself.

Finally he reached the edge of the forest. Pausing to catch his breath, he looked to either side of the tiny inlet to make sure nobody was around. He saw no one. From the south side of the point came the sound of distant voices. The Bentons were still combing the area, looking for him. So long as the outboard motor started right away, though, their chances of escape were good.

He bent over and grabbed the bow rail again when a familiar voice called out, "Yo, headerball. Where do yeh think yer going?"

Mason let go of the rail and jerked around to see Murph step out from behind a tree. Instinctively, he reached down to his Sig P226 by his waist.

"Forget it," Murph warned him, pointing his Glock at Mason's chest. "Or yer a dead man."

"I'm a dead man anyway." Nevertheless, Mason took his hand away from his holster. He stared at Murph. "How the hell did you find me? No one knew where this boat was other than Doney, and he's dead."

"A stroke of luck really. I saw you and Doney hide the boat here the other day. When yeh disappeared into the forest, I figured yeh were probably heading here." Murph grinned. "Looks like I took the shortcut too. I've been waiting bleedin' ages for yeh."

"Mason, what's going on?" Tania had been staring in amazement from one man to the other. With everything that had been happening, Mason hadn't yet had a chance to tell her about Murph's treachery. "We need to go. Whatever is going on between you two, save it till later."

Mason shook his head. "He's not on our side, Tania," he said, unable to keep the bitterness out of his tone. "He betrayed us and struck a deal with the Bentons. Killed everyone at the main checkpoint and let them into the camp."

Tania's mouth dropped even farther. "I-I don't understand, Murph" she stuttered. "Mason treated you good. He had plans for you. Why would you do such a thing?"

Despite everything, it was the question burning most on Mason's mind right now too.

"Pretty simple, really." Murph took another step forward, watching Mason warily. "See, I'm a Benton man through and through, only I got stranded here that night you took the camp. Gatto was just too dumb to figure it out. So were you, for that matter."

Everything suddenly became clear to Mason. "It wasn't Gatto who set me up yesterday, was it?" he said hoarsely. "It was you."

Murph nodded. "Thought I was a goner too, when you pointed yer pistol at me through the seats. Doney looked like he was about to figure it out, only yeh shut him up." He blew a mock sigh of relief. "Should have listened to him, Mason. He was onto me."

Deep at the center of Mason's brain, a violent storm started to brew. Murph had played him for a fool. How could he have been so stupid?

Murph glanced quickly over at Tania, still holding Mason's rifle awkwardly in her grip. "Right, love, drop that rifle on the ground. No one's going to hurt yeh, I promise. As for you, Mason, thumb and forefinger on the butt of yer pistol and ease it out of that holster. Just like they do in the movies."

The rage in Mason's head reached its peak. Waves of white heat shot across his frontal lobes, searing the backs of his eyeballs. He reached his hand down to his waist, staring at Tania intently as he did so, willing his intentions into her head.

She caught his gaze and a look of pure fear flashed across her face. Then she did the thing that Mason most needed her to do. Arms trembling, she raised the Heckler to her chest and swung the barrel over in Murph's direction.

"No, Tania!" Murph yelled. At that same moment, Mason grabbed his Sig and pulled it free from its holster.

Two shots rang out in quick succession.

One of them, the .45 ACP round from Murph's Glock, thudded into Mason's chest, sending a shockwave throughout his entire body. Time slowed down, slower than he'd ever experienced before. He looked across at Tania to see a red mist spray out the side of her neck. The MR556 slipped from her grasp and tumbled to the ground in front of her.

From behind a nearby tree, a small blonde woman wearing fatigues stepped out, a semi-automatic rifle in her grip, still pointing at Tania.

Tania's mouth gaped open like she was trying to tell Mason something. She staggered toward him, but after a couple of steps she stumbled and fell to the ground. Lying on her side, her body convulsed a few times, then remained still.

From somewhere deep inside his shattered body, Mason mustered the last of his rage. "Muurrphh!" he roared, raising his pistol.

The girl swiveled her rifle across at him and shot him twice more in the chest. Mason staggered backward and the pistol dropped from his grip.

"Hey, asshole, his name isn't Murph," the girl said. "It's Jonah. And he's my husband."

As the light faded from his eyes, Mason stumbled over to Tania's slain figure. His knees buckled and he tumbled on top of her. He was dead before he hit the ground.

***

Jonah stepped forward, his pistol pointing down at Mason's giant frame. It lay halfway across Tania's body, and her bloodied face stuck out from one side at an angle.

He looked over at Colleen and shook his head. "Why did she go and do that? I don't think she ever handled a weapon in her life before. Total madness."

Colleen came over to stand beside him and stared down at the two bodies. "Why do you care?" she asked. "I don't feel sorry for her. She must have known everything Mason was up to."

Despite all Jonah had endured recently, the sight of Tania's frail figure crumpled on the ground affected him. He was amazed by the loyalty she'd shown Mason. "I couldn't rightly tell yeh," he said quietly. "Just doesn't seem right." He turned his head away. "Come on, let's get out of here. I've seen enough dead bodies to last me a bleedin' lifetime."

CHAPTER 41

That afternoon, nine people sat around the table in the Benton Survivors Group council room. Sheriff Rollins held the chair with the four members of his council to his right, while on the left, sat the four members of the Eastwood War Committee.

A discussion was in progress regarding what to do with the remnants of Mason's crew, who had surrendered earlier. Several were badly wounded, and at least two wouldn't survive the night. Eight had been killed, while it was estimated that about a dozen had managed to escape from the headland. The question now was, what to do with the eleven remaining prisoners.

There were no easy solutions. One thing was for sure: they couldn't keep them locked up for long. Guarding so many was a strain on their resources. Soon they would have to start feeding them too.

"No choice," Henry Perter said. "We got to let them go. I mean, what else are we to do, shoot them all?"

"Why not?" Mary Sadowski replied. "That's what we did with Russ."

Perter stared at her in amazement. "Mary, that was just one person. Russ tortured Ned and was proven to be complicit in murdering three of our men, along with several others. We have no idea the exact crimes of any of these men. Besides, some of them are badly injured. What are we going to do—execute them in chairs?"

Mary's face indicated that was exactly what she felt they should do. "These men murdered young Marcus…and Bob and Joe. Then they invaded our camp, where we lost six more people, plus the two today." She stared at Perter fiercely. "Tell me, Hank, what do you think people like that are going to do if we let them go?"

"I-I don't rightly know," Perter stuttered weakly.

"You don't know?" Ralph said. He sat at the end of the table, his gangly legs stretched out in front of him. "Let me tell you something. I *do* know. They'll pick a new leader, then continue on as before. Find other victims to prey on along the lake shore. Kill, rob, plunder, rape. It won't matter to them. Once a man loses his soul, it don't come back anytime soon, if ever. Take that from a man who spent fifteen years in a cage."

"Exactly," Mary said, giving Ralph an approving nod. "You really want to be responsible for what these animals go on and do?" she asked, facing Perter again.

He looked at her uneasily. "No, but if it comes to lining them up against a wall and shooting them, you can count me out. That's too rich for my tastes."

"We all respect that, Hank," Ned Granger said gently to his friend. "Nonetheless, I don't think we'll be short of volunteers for the firing squad."

"Damn straight," Bert Olvan growled. "I'll show no mercy to those murdering bastards. Bob Harper was a good friend of mine. I knew him the best part of ten years."

"All right," Rollins cut in. He looked around the table. "Other than Hank, is there anyone else who has a moral objection to executing these men?" All hands at the table remained down. "Well, that's settled then. After the meeting, I'll put together a list of volunteers and we'll draw lots for the firing squad."

"When do we execute them?" Walter asked.

"Why wait? Let's be done with it now," Clete said. "Waiting is no good to us *or* them."

"No point in delaying things," Rollins agreed. "This afternoon we'll take them down to the beach a few at a time and execute them." He grimaced. "Not a pleasant task. Then again, these aren't pleasant times."

***

Outside Chickasaw, Jonah Murphy leaned both arms over the porch rail. Beer in hand, he stared out across the water with a distant, weary expression. The last few days had taken their toll, and a somber mood hung over him. Though earlier he'd already whispered a brief thanks to the fellow upstairs, he intended having a proper talk with him later, rattle off the last of the Hail Mary's he'd promised him. Perhaps that might help.

He straightened up and poked his head inside the cabin, where Colleen was unpacking her clothes. Earlier, he had gone around the back of the cabin and into the woods to retrieve her backpack. Colleen's eyes had lit up when she'd seen it. It saved her the bother of having to restock all her camping attire again.

"Jonah, are you all right?" she asked, looking over at him worriedly where he leaned against the door frame, staring out vacantly. "I don't think I ever seen you this quiet before."

He gave her a weak smile. "I'm fine. I think everything over the past few days is finally catching up with me, that's all."

Colleen nodded. "It's been a terrible strain on all of us, especially you." she smiled at him. "I'm so proud of you. You know that, don't you?"

Jonah's expression grew serious. "I did it for you, love. I mean, I like the Bentons and all that, but the reason I stayed behind was to help keep you safe. I just never thought I'd get so much blood on me hands in the process." He reflected a moment. "Matt and them three other geezers that night, then Gatto's crew…and…and poor old Pauly. He really didn't deserve that." A haunted look came over his face. "It…it gets to you, yeh know?"

Colleen walked around from the closet and stood in front of him. "I know, but you're strong. You'll get over it," she said firmly.

"Yeah, give me a day or two and I'll be back to me old self." Jonah paused briefly. "I tell yeh something, though, I'm a bit cheesed off with Bert. To be honest, I've got the right hump with him."

Colleen looked at him blankly. "What on Earth for? I thought you two were great pals. Especially since he spent every day at Devil's Point keeping in contact with you."

Jonah hesitated. "He's a dead-on bloke, I just didn't like the way he used you to make sure I went along with the plan today. That was low."

"What are you talking about, Jonah?"

Jonah went on to explain how the previous day, Olvan had told him how Colleen had insisted on being involved in Operation Blitzkrieg. He felt certain she'd been manipulated by Olvan to ensure his cooperation.

Colleen shook her head firmly. "It wasn't like that. Soon as I heard about the plan to take back the camp, I volunteered to join Mary's team. Nobody made me do anything."

"You sure?"

"Absolutely positive. It had nothing to do with Bert."

Jonah relaxed. "Grand, then Bertie's in me good bukes again. I feel bad now. I gave him a bit of a frosty stare earlier. Never mind, I'll make it up to him later over a beer."

He looked across at the shelf space, where Colleen had almost finished putting her stuff away. "Nice job," he said. "I feel something's missing though."

Colleen frowned. "I don't think so."

Jonah bounded over to his own rucksack on the far side of the room and pulled out a frilly pink negligee and a pair of matching high heels. He grinned. "These look familiar to you?"

"My god, Jonah! You still got those?" Colleen exclaimed, laughing hard. "I don't believe it!"

"Too bleedin' right. Kept them hidden at the bottom of me pack all this time. Didn't want Mason thinking I liked to wear them meself. I don't think that would have gone down too well."

He walked around to the closet and placed them on top of her pile of clothes. "Tonight, I'll fish out a bottle of wine and get a couple of candles going while you slip into yer hot stuff. You good for that?"

Collen stepped over to him and put her arms around his waist, drawing herself up close to him. "Oh, I'm *real* good for that," she murmured softly in his ear. "Make sure you get candles that last all night long."

Jonah could feel the unrelenting pressure of the last few days starting to lift. He rubbed his hands gleefully. "You know, love, I think I'm starting to feel better already. I can feel it in me bones!"

FROM THE AUTHOR

For sneak peaks, updates on new releases and bonus content, subscribe to my mailing list at www.mikesheridanbooks.com.

THE MILITIA (working title), Book 4 in the NO DIRECTION HOME series is out October 2017.

Made in the USA
Columbia, SC
13 October 2017